ONE GOLDEN SUMMER

HELEN ROW TOEWS

One Golden Summer
Copyright 2022 by Helen Row Toews
All rights reserved.
This book, or any portion thereof, may not be reproduced or used in any manner whatsoever without the express written permission of the author, except for the use of brief quotations in a book review.

Printed in North America
First edition, 2023

Edited by Under Wraps Publishing
Cover by MiblArt

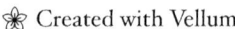 Created with Vellum

CHAPTER 1

"Sorry Angelina, but I'm going to have to let you go." Glenn Sudbury spoke forcefully, as though expecting an argument. He took off his cap and dragged an arm over his dripping brow, avoiding her eyes.

She'd known something was up when he had hurried out to meet her the moment she parked her truck in the lot. By the time she climbed out and locked it for the night, he was there. Now, they stood together in the gravel. Her, shading her eyes against the setting sun of a long day's work, and he, shifting uncomfortably from one foot to the other.

"Go?" she said. "Go where exactly?" Lifting her ponytail of long black hair, she flipped it off her neck. It was hot and Angelina was tired. She swung her coat and lunch bag over to the other arm and tried to understand.

Glenn stared over her left shoulder as he replaced his hat and continued in a loud monotone that sounded rehearsed. "You've worked hard for this company over the last six years, and I appreciate it, but management has fielded several complaints about your driving this week," he shrugged and looked away. "You've become a liability I can't afford."

"A liability?" she repeated. It was finally sinking in. "You're firing me?" Her voice rose and she took an unsteady step back, shaking her head. The things she was carrying dropped to her feet, unheeded. "I've done my very best for this company and love my..." she began.

"Not firing—exactly," he interrupted in a strained voice. "But I've received reports that you've taken risks with a loaded truck and shown a disregard for traffic laws. This company has zero tolerance for that sort of thing and a clean accident record. I can't afford to lose it now." He was choosing to ignore her last remark. "Anyway, it's more like laying you off," he added.

Glenn's eyes flicked to meet hers, then slid away. He bent to pick up the items she'd dropped, shoved them into her arms and turned on his heel, signaling the end of their discussion. She stood in a stunned silence.

"You'll get two weeks' severance pay in the mail," he called back over his shoulder. "Clear out your truck and leave the keys on my desk." He crunched across the driveway to where other trucks were parked behind a chain-link fence and disappeared from view.

Angelina couldn't believe it. Shock rooted her to the spot. She'd been fired. Kicked out. Told to get her things and clear off. She shook her head again, trying to make sense of the absurdness of it all. But a voice inside her head told her it made perfect sense. And it had *nothing* to do with her driving.

Kenton. That snivelling little jerk! As she collected

herself and marched back to grab her sunglasses and extra sweater from the truck, she relived the last two weeks of work.

Kenton, the boss' son, had returned from university and lost no time in swaggering around his father's gravel hauling business like he owned the place. He was there each afternoon issuing heavy-handed orders to the office staff, riding along with the drivers to tell them how to do a job most of them had done for thirty years, and making a general nuisance of himself.

He was full of his own importance, looking to take over the family business with zero understanding of how to run it or treat employees with respect. To top it off, he was encouraged by a father who was blind to his son's faults. Angelina suspected it started when Glenn's wife had died, leaving him to raise the boy alone. Even now, the young man could do no wrong.

Still, apart from doing her best to avoid him, she'd thought nothing of it until she noticed him watching her with a predatory look that caused her to cringe. He was trouble. Twice he'd asked her for a date after a safety meeting, which she rebuffed with a smile.

"You're too young for me," she'd joked, sidling for the door. "Are you even twenty yet?" His father had overheard the exchange, she was sure of it. Yet the man had shot Angelina a look of annoyance. Had Glenn really expected her to accept the advances of a kid ten years younger than herself, just because of who he was?

However, her refusals didn't deter Kenton, they seemed to make him even more persistent. Then, one day, things had gotten worse. She grimaced in remembrance.

He'd climbed into the truck beside her, announcing he was coming along to 'assess her skill set.' She'd felt more than a prickle of alarm. But how could she refuse the boss' son when his father was standing behind him, grinning with pride like the Cheshire Cat? After all, her fears were nothing more than suspicions born of women's intuition. She resolved to ignore him and get on with her job.

She was carrying a heavy load of sand bound for a paving company outside of town and needed her wits about her. As she drove past city limits and began to gear up, he made his move.

"Angelina, baby, you have a body that could drive a man wild," Kenton crooned. Unbuckling his seatbelt, he slithered across the bench seat and slipped an arm around her shoulders.

"What do you think you're doing?" she ground out between gritted teeth. "Stay away from me Kenton, I'm not interested!"

"I think you're wrong. I've seen the signs...besides, I'm pretty irresistible. You and I could have a lot of fun together this summer, baby. Just think about it." He leaned in to nuzzle her ear. Angelina's throat constricted as a wave of cheap, nauseating cologne rolled past her nostrils. Keeping her eyes on the road, she used one arm to push him away.

"Kenton! No! I just want to do my job, okay? Get back to your side of the cab like a good boy."

"I say the attraction is mutual, you just don't know it yet." He pulled back for a moment and looked at her hungrily, like an animal eyeing its prey.

Angelina glanced at him with a scowl. His face was

flushed and determined, his breathing rapid. He was almost salivating, for heaven's sake!

"I told you I'm *not* interested and I'm warning you to leave me alone."

Kenton didn't listen. His hands grasped for her again, this time he touched her breast. Angelina's stomach churned with revulsion. She whacked his arm away while keeping her eyes on the road.

Braking suddenly, she felt the load of sand shift forward, and took a deep breath to calm herself lest she cause a problem with the truck. Then, Angelina geared down before cranking the wheel and sending them into a driveway that wasn't part of the route. She stopped and reversed out to head back the way she'd come.

Kenton slammed against his door with these unexpected moves, and then fell against the dash. "Where do ya think you're goin'?" he hollered. "You have a job to finish. And that wasn't safe." The hungry look was replaced with an angry one. He straightened and made a show of dusting himself off.

She remained grim and silent, focused on taking Kenton back to his father. The kid was going to cause an accident and she wouldn't risk it by putting up with his harassment.

"Fine," he yelled. "You take me back to the shop. I got something I need to tell my dad, *the boss*," he sneered. After that he was sullen and silent, sitting with his arms crossed and a foul look on his face.

When Angelina pulled through the gate and up to the office, he didn't even wait till she stopped. Kenton threw open the door and jumped to the ground before slamming it closed.

Good, she'd thought. She was furious with the little creep and only too glad to be rid of him, but that's when the complaints over her driving began. Glenn had called her into his office that night after work and explained that someone had called in to report she'd been involved in a near collision. Angelina knew exactly who had complained. Though knowing her work ethic, she'd thought his father would have been too sensible to fall for it.

Apparently not.

Angelina came back to the present with a sigh. She stroked a hand along the dashboard of the truck that had been like her second home for the past six years. It felt as though she were leaving an old friend.

Sure, after high school she'd worked the sort of jobs that were what her parents had expected. She'd even spent three long years in business college, taking an office administration course, but it wasn't where her heart was. That year she'd spent working as an executive secretary in a law firm had left her feeling dry as dust. It just wasn't for her.

Angelina loved driving. The feeling of escaping four walls while the wind whistled past her face through an open window was exhilarating. She loved shifting through the gears and the thrill of knowing she could handle the large vehicles that were traditionally considered a man's domain. It was unconventional, but it was her.

Pulling her sunglasses off the dash, she took one last look to make sure she had everything. She slid out, slammed the door, and rushed to throw her things inside her own vehicle before heading into the office to toss the truck keys on Glenn's desk.

Emerging moments later, Angelina paused. A couple of the guys she worked with were striding toward her, concern written on their faces.

"Hey, tell me it's not true?" Garry, the first to reach her, bent down to search her face. "Glenn just told us this is your last day."

She shrugged. "It's true alright."

"It was Kenton, wasn't it? I overheard him talking about you in an...unpleasant way." Mark, a grizzled man in his sixties, slammed a fist into his palm. "Do you want us to do something about it? We have no problem confronting Glenn and I'd take particular pleasure in chatting with Kenton." His face darkened with anger.

Garry nodded in agreement. "That boy needs a tune-up for sure." He turned to peer through the office door. "Is he in there? I'd like to have a *word* with him myself."

Angelina smiled with wobbly lips, blinking rapidly. "No. You guys are great, and I appreciate the offer, but that would only get you fired too. I couldn't stay here anyway. Not now."

She investigated the faces of these men who'd given her a hard time when she first started working for the company. 'A girl,' they'd said with a certain amount of contempt, 'pretending to drive a truck in a man's world.'

It hadn't been easy in the beginning, but she'd persevered, done her job, and done it well. She'd won their admiration and respect. It meant a lot to her, and she hated to leave this way. However, she didn't want to be around Kenton, and Glenn appeared blind to his son's flaws.

"It's okay, really it is," she said. Acting on impulse, she gave them both a hug. "You take care of yourselves and watch out for Kenton, he's dangerous." She flipped her ponytail behind her, took a deep breath, and forced herself to grin. "I'll be fine. Maybe a break is just what I need."

ANGELINA COLLAPSED AT THE KITCHEN TABLE IN HER apartment and bent to untie her steel-toed work boots. She kicked them aside. *Won't need those for a while.* A knife twisted in her chest as she wondered who would hire her now. She was worried that the supposed driving incidents she had, coupled with the false complaints, would follow her and mar her driving record whether they were true or not. Would Glenn do that to her? She didn't trust the man any longer.

It had taken a long time to even be hired at that company. She was a woman, had no previous work history, wasn't taken seriously in this world still dominated by men, and knew she didn't look the truck-driver part. Glenn had told her she looked too young and was far too inexperienced. Of course, wearing a red frilly dress and heels to that first interview had been a stupid idea. On top of all the other drawbacks, she'd looked too *pretty*. That wasn't conceit talking, she knew, it was just a fact.

However, she'd always taken pains with her appearance. Once she got the job, there wasn't any reason she should let herself go just because she drove trucks for a living. True, wearing makeup, a nice pair of jeans, blouse, and bright red lipstick every day earned her the mockery of the men she worked with. But in time they'd stopped whistling and teasing, and accepted her as a professional who knew her way around a truck.

Angelina padded across the kitchen and opened the refrigerator. Where was that Moscato? She moved ketchup, a day-old Greek salad, and a large container of yogurt before wrapping her fingers around an almost-full bottle of wine and pulling it forth. Grabbing a glass, she carried both into her tiny living room. It felt good to flop onto the sofa and put her feet up.

She rested her head back among the pillows, lifting the icy glass to take a sip. The soothing liquid trickled down her throat. With a sigh, Angelina closed her eyes and tried to block out the last few hours.

It was not to be. Her cell phone sprang to life, alternating between fits of beeping and vibrating on the table where she'd left her boots. She disregarded it, and a smile crossed her lips as it stopped. As the sound started again, she froze, the buzzing so insistent that the phone toppled from the table and clattered to the floor.

"*Damn!*" Angelina set her glass beside the lamp at her elbow. Jumping up she ran to retrieve the frantic technology. *Who was it? Aah, it figures.* She stared at the number as she swiped a finger across to answer the call.

"Hi Mom."

"Hello honey. What's wrong?" her mother's voice floated into the room as Angelina set the phone on speaker, placed it beside her wine, and dropped into the comfort of her cushions once more.

"You can't possibly think something's wrong from two words." Angelina rolled her eyes. How did the woman know? Sixth sense? Mother's intuition? Dumb luck?

"I can hear it in your voice. Are you alright?"

Her mother's concern almost released the tears that were ready to flow. Before Angelina spoke again, she drew a deep breath and steadied herself. Might as well get it over with sooner than later.

"I was—let go today."

"What! Why?"

Angelina summed it up in as few words as possible, then reached for her wine and thumped her feet onto the coffee table again.

"Oh sweetheart, I'm sorry. That's so unfair." Her mother clucked her tongue, and despite herself, Angelina smiled. She'd seen her mom do it a thousand times.

"I'd like you to come over here for supper." Mom was using her 'no argument' voice. "That's the reason I was calling you. Marcie and Alec are driving out from the city, and they asked specifically that you be present. Your sister has some big announcement to share with us."

Angelina could feel her mother's sympathy like a warm embrace and loved her for it. Except she didn't feel like facing her family tonight and going through the whole miserable tale again. She wanted to lick her wounds in private. Just her, the bottle of wine, and perhaps that hefty bar of chocolate she'd stashed in the cupboard last payday.

"No thanks Mom. Tell them I'm sorry, but I can't do it tonight." She dragged a tattered old blanket from the back of the sofa and picked at the tufts.

"Getting out of your apartment is the best thing," her mother insisted. "Don't argue, Dad will come get you. I'm sending him to the store for parsley anyhow. Be ready in fifteen minutes." She hung up.

Again, Angelina rolled her eyes. Her mom meant well, she knew that, but the woman couldn't leave well enough alone. Reaching for her glass, Angelina downed what was left and poured herself another. If she had to go, she wasn't changing for the event, apart from her shoes, of course. They could take her as she was, a thirty-year-old truck-driver with faded lipstick and a black mark on her reputation.

DAD REACHED FOR HER HAND AND SQUEEZED IT TIGHT as he pulled into the driveway and turned off the car. Apart from a hug at the door, he hadn't asked her a thing about the trouble she'd had that day. She appreciated it.

"I know you wanted to stay home," he said, looking into her eyes and smiling ruefully. "But maybe it will do you some good to be with people who love you."

With a final squeeze, he let her go, pulled the baseball cap he always wore lower over his thinning hair, and climbed out. Her father, Mark, was a tall, slim man. Since

Sharon, Angelina's mother, was plump and petite, it had always been accepted that it was from her father that Angelina had gotten her height of 5'8". However, Dad had a slight stoop now from years of hard work on the family farm. It had been sold when he retired due to ill health.

That was when they'd moved into town and purchased a cozy bungalow with a pretty white veranda. It was smaller than the house they'd had on the farm, but they both enjoyed being closer to friends and having more time to spend with family.

Rounding the hood, Dad beckoned to her and then, as she didn't move, he walked over to open her door. Accepting his outstretched arm, she allowed herself to be helped from the vehicle and led into the garage.

Despite her protests, she'd taken the time to change into clean jeans and a green mossy-coloured silk blouse that matched her eyes. She had released her hair from its elastic, brushed it out, and reapplied lipstick. But she didn't feel any better for it. Her feet dragged as they mounted the steps and prepared to enter the kitchen.

Her mother flung open the door, short, dark curls bouncing as she enveloped her daughter in a long embrace. Her green eyes, the same shade as Angelina's own, reflected the sympathy she felt. Angelina's sister Marcie followed close behind to throw her arms around the pair. They stood together for a long moment before pulling Angelina into the room where the delicious aroma of roast beef filled her senses. She breathed deep. It was home and her family's love was palpable. Maybe she did feel a little better.

Angelina looked around the inviting kitchen, a sense of comfort flooding over her. She and mom had painted the kitchen a bright, cheery yellow before her parents moved in. Then, her dad had installed new white cupboards along with an updated countertop. Together the three of them had chosen stainless steel appliances to complete the fresh new look.

Over the sink, a south-facing window, hung with pale blue curtains, looked out into the back garden. Since Dad was the official dish washer, he often remarked it did his heart good to look out at the flower beds and vegetable patch as he worked.

A long table sat at the center of the space. Beyond that was the living room where deep, comfy sofas invited guests to stay awhile, and a huge television set graced the wall.

"I'm *so* excited you came!" Marcie burst out. "Mom told me what happened, and I think that stinks, but it couldn't have come at a better time!"

Angelina looked down at her sister's flushed, grinning face and realised something momentous had taken place. Marcie had more of their father's features and sandy-coloured hair and their mother's build. Angelina smiled, and then squealed in surprise as, despite her diminutive stature, Marcie grabbed her around the waist and almost lifted her off her feet as they twirled about the kitchen.

"What is it?" Angelina demanded, laughing. Marcie slowed, let go and bent over to catch her breath. Her husband, Alec, nodded with encouragement, beaming from the hallway. Their parents watching, joined hands in anticipation.

Straightening, Marcie threw her arms in the air. "I'm pregnant!" she screeched. "We found out today."

"Wow." Angelina was dumbfounded. "That's fantastic!"

For the last five years, Marcie and Alec had tried to have a baby. Recently they'd seen doctors and specialists, but no one had offered any reasons for the problem, or any solutions. Now, this wonderful news—an answered prayer. Angelina grabbed Marcie again, held her close and kissed both her cheeks; the wetness of her sister's tears mingling with her own.

"I'm so happy for you both," she said. Moving to Alec, she hugged him too and then the whole family met in the center of the kitchen to share in the joy.

When they all stepped apart to blow noses and mop faces, Marcie linked arms with her fair-haired husband and spoke again.

"I have more news and it affects you directly, Angel."

That had always been Marcie's pet name for her little sister. Angelina turned, listening for what could possibly add to the happiness the two had already shared.

"There's more?" their mother said in bewilderment. "What? You won the lottery?" She dropped into a chair and fanned her face with a bunched up tea towel.

Marcie nodded with barely suppressed glee. "Sort of. I've got a ticket to France in my purse that I won't be using. I can't take any risks now." She glanced up at her husband and patted her tummy. "I want you to have it, Angel, and take the trip I'd planned. Is your passport current?"

Angelina nodded, the grin fading from her face.

"Great. There are a few other details I'll have to tell you about too, and we'll have to pay a fee to have it transferred to your name, but this is perfect! I was going to beg you to ask for a holiday to go. But thanks to that idiot at your workplace, you now have unlimited time."

Angelina felt dazed. *France?*

"When?" she asked weakly. "Why? And I *don't* have unlimited time. I have bills to pay, same as you."

"Tomorrow!" Marcie whooped, ignoring the latter part of Angelina's statement. "I'll explain everything as I help you pack."

"Pack? I'm *not* leaving for France tomorrow. Are you crazy?" Angelina laughed, but there was a hysterical edge to her voice. She paused, watching, and waiting for her sister to agree, but it didn't happen.

"You can't be serious?" When both Marcie and Alec nodded, affirming it was true, Angelina slumped onto a chair beside her mother. Dad leaned against a counter listening intently, but saying nothing.

"Here," her mother tossed the tea towel to her daughter. "You need this more than I do."

Angelina's hands shook as she lifted the damp cloth and began to beat the air in front of her face.

"We're perfectly serious," Alec said, moving to pull out a chair and sit beside his sister-in-law. He spoke earnestly, leaning forward and searching Angelina's face with concern. "It's a bit of an involved story. Marcie was planning to meet your cousin, Sarah, in Montreal tomorrow morning and fly to Paris in the afternoon. Sarah's been there visiting some family on her father's side, and apparently made friends with a mother and son who are in Canada on holiday from France. They asked Sarah to go back with them and to invite a friend if she wanted."

"Why haven't I heard of this until now?" Mom questioned in a reproachful voice.

Marcie looked sheepish. "I didn't think you'd approve."

"Nonsense. I'd like to go to France myself," Sharon announced, grinning. "What do you say Mark? Maybe *I* should go with Sarah?"

"I couldn't possibly get along here without you," her husband responded, crossing the linoleum to lay a hand on either of Sharon's shoulders. He bent to kiss the top of her head.

She patted his hand. "Of course, I won't go anywhere, but someone needs to keep an eye on that young girl."

Angelina paused in her frantic fluttering and looked at her sister. "So...what's the catch? Why you? No offense, but I can't imagine you'd be Sarah's first choice as a friend to take to France."

Marcie giggled. "I knew you'd be suspicious." She stepped to the table and sat on Angelina's other side with a huff of air. "Honey, could you get me a drink?" she asked her husband. As he rose, she smoothed her blue cotton dress over her knees and took a breath.

"I was going along because I'm worried about Sarah. She's only just turned nineteen and is quite naïve, as you know. I don't know these people, and that concerned both Aunt Esther and me. It sounds like Sarah has fallen for this French fellow and figures he'll ask her to marry him. A similar situation happened last summer. Remember?"

Angelina remembered. The whole family had lived

in fear until the girl had been found living in a garden shed somewhere in Montana.

Marcie braided her fingers together and for the first time since she'd arrived, Angelina saw a shadow cross her sister's face.

"I don't believe these people asked Sarah to visit although she raves about their kindness, and they did pay for both plane tickets," Marcie clasped her hands. "I think she foisted herself upon them, but she won't be dissuaded. All that aside, Aunt Esther begged me to go along and keep an eye on her."

Marcie shrugged at Angelina's doubtful expression and explained further. "Sarah liked the idea of me coming since I'm married and, in her mind, wouldn't be competing for the guy's attention. I'm sure he's wealthy which prompted her grand ideas of marriage. I sincerely doubt he has the slightest inclination of doing so. My fear is that he plans on having a fling with her and then throw her aside. Anyway, I couldn't refuse. It was a two-week holiday to France, and someone must go with Sarah. Who could say no?"

"Me." Angelina spoke with emphasis. "The incongruity of the situation defies understanding. I mean, I'd love to go to France...but contrary to popular belief, this isn't as great a time for me as you seem to think."

"Oh, I know," Marcie caught one of Angelina's hands and pressed it between her own. "It's been a horrible day for you. But look at the bright side—"

"The bright side?" Angelina interrupted with a shout. "There's no bright side to being fired for something you didn't do."

"Okay...well maybe I didn't choose the right words.

But you have to admit, suddenly you have no responsibilities and there's no one in your life to keep you here." Marcie spoke encouragingly, clearly not realizing that what she said was having a negative effect on her only sibling.

Angelina stared at the floor. Marcie was right. She had no one in her life and no job to prevent her from going, but hearing it spoken so casually, hurt.

It had been three months since Bryan had left town without warning or even a backward glance her way. After dating for a year, they'd talked about making things permanent and settling down. She'd deserved more than to be dumped without so much as a word of explanation. Since then, Angelina had shut herself off, vowing she was finished with men and their treacherous ways for good. Today had only solidified that belief further.

"You know what," she said, standing up and tossing the cloth aside, "I'll do it. Someone has to protect Sarah from this guy...or, knowing Sarah, maybe the guy will need protection from her. Anyway, who better for the job than me."

CHAPTER 2

Angelina stood up with the rest of the passengers on the flight from Edmonton, Alberta, to Montreal, Quebec, and grasped her carry-on luggage before making her way down the aisle and off the plane. She tried in vain to push the wrinkles out of the wide-leg khaki capris and white tee she'd chosen to wear. With a matching jacket, the outfit made an attractive, yet comfortable ensemble for travelling.

Reaching the terminal's restaurant area, she adjusted her backpack into a more comfortable position and stepped to one side, allowing people to hurry past her as she consulted her phone. Sarah was supposed to have texted by now, but the cell phone registered nothing.

Sighing, Angelina started walking, keeping watch for somewhere she could get a good coffee.

"Angelina!" cried an excited voice. "Over here."

Whirling around, Angelina saw Sarah push a suitcase aside and, when it toppled over in front of her, leap over it to rush across the lounge. The people she was with remained seated.

"I'm, like, *so* happy you're here," the girl gushed, as she flung her arms around Angelina's shoulders. Then, lowering her voice, she whispered, "Do you see that hot guy I'm with? He's *so* cute and he has piles of money. I just know we're going to be together. I want you to watch for signs that he loves me, okay?"

Angelina drew back from Sarah with a laugh and held the young woman at arm's length. Marcie's fears were not unfounded.

"I'm glad to see you too, honey," she said. Sarah was even prettier than Angelina remembered. Her curly blonde hair had been trimmed into a stylish bob, a light scattering of freckles dusted her nose, and big blue eyes regarded Angelina with complete seriousness. She wore a fitted, one-piece romper of light blue with a pattern of tiny pink flowers dotting the material and had added a touch of gloss in the same colour to her lips. She was delectable and innocent. Angelina scowled in the direction of the 'hot guy' and mentally armed herself. Her job started now.

"Why don't you introduce me?" Angelina's voice sounded like steel and Sarah glanced at her with a frown forming between her eyes.

"Okay..." With a toss of her curls, Sarah linked their arms and led them across the busy aisle. The man she'd been sitting with, rose to his feet. "Angelina, this is Julien Belliveau. Julien, this is my *older* cousin, Angelina." All of a sudden, she sounded very formal. The girl leaned toward Julien to add. "My mom and her mom are sisters."

The emphasis on *older* wasn't lost on Angelina, but she was fine with that. She *was* older, and hopefully wiser, as this man would soon discover. In watching him stand, she wouldn't have been surprised if he'd clicked his heels together as he stiffly came to attention. He looked very—put together, and she remembered, with a pang, where she'd spilled coffee on her t-shirt that morning.

"I'm pleased to meet you," she said, stepping forward to extend her hand with a forced smile. Unfortunately, her rubber-soled wedges caught in the carpeting. She lost her footing, only saving herself from a fall by involuntarily reaching out with both hands and splaying them against Julien's chest.

"Yikes!" she shrieked as his own hands came forward to steady her. "Please forgive me." She glared down at the floor as though the carpet was at fault.

"*Pas de problème.*" He answered in French and bent down to look in her face. "Are you alright?"

"Y-yes, of course. I'm fine," she stammered. What a foolish thing to do. Mentally she kicked herself for her clumsiness.

Her eyes met gray ones without wavering as she struggled to gather herself. She'd purposely worn her highest wedge heels with this meeting in mind and now it had come to ruin. She already enjoyed an elevated height, but wanted the additional stature that a few more centimetres would provide. Her plan was to look this man in the eye and hold his gaze. Falling into his arms had *not* been a part of her strategy.

He was far taller than her, even in her heels. She thought perhaps 6'3" and not bad looking either. His sandy-coloured hair was cut short on the sides, but was longer on top and brushed straight up to fall over his forehead. A few flecks of silver at the temples told her he was at least in his mid-thirties. He had several-days growth of a moustache and beard on his rugged face. He looked casual, but still well-dressed in jeans and a white button-up. His eyes narrowed as they met hers and he grasped her hand in a powerful grip. Not to be outdone, she gripped him back.

"*Enchante*," he said, inclining his head. If he was surprised at her firm handshake, he made no sign of it. Letting go, he turned to include his mother in the introduction. "And I would like you to meet *ma mere,* Elyse Belleveau."

Angelina swivelled her attention to the mother, who didn't look more than fifty-five. She was petite and slim, an attractive woman with impeccably done makeup. She wore a chic, cream, monochromatic blouse paired with tailored trousers, and had shoulder-length, chestnut-coloured hair.

Planting her feet solidly, and extending her hand once more, Angelina wasn't taking any chances this time. She smiled warmly as they shook and was rewarded with genuine friendliness.

"*Enchante.*" Elyse repeated the French word and followed it up with the meaning. "So nice to meet you." The lady paused after each word, and they were delivered in a much thicker accent than that of her son. Angelina got the impression his mother didn't know much English and had only learned the phrase in order to use it at times like this.

"It's lovely to meet you as well." Angelina took a

step back and untangled her arms from her backpack, allowing it to swing free as she looked again for a coffee shop. She could feel Julien's hard gray-blue eyes boring into her soul, or so it felt, and hastily moved further away, needing space and time to think. The silence that had fallen between them was already strained.

"Will you sit down?" Julien asked, ducking his head to indicate the seat next to Sarah. You are seated in first class with us." Angelina shook her head as though to clear cobwebs. His accent was quite captivating.

"Oh," she said, feeling colour rush into her face. "You didn't have to do that Mr. B—"

"Julien," he interrupted smoothly.

"Right. Well, you didn't need to do that, Julien," Angelina closed her eyes as she stumbled over his first name. "I could have sat on my own in the economy section without suffering any harm." She forced another smile to soften her words, but secretly was cursing under her breath. It would have been nice to be alone for the voyage.

"Of course, you would not be harmed," he said with irritating cheer. "Yet, I thought you might want to sit with your *plus jeune cousine, n'est-ce pas?*" With an expressive shrug of his broad shoulders, Julien turned the question into more of a statement. There was almost a hint of a smile in his words and Angelina shot him a look. However, he stooped to set Sarah's luggage upright and Angelina was left to think she had only imagined it.

Fortunately, she had studied French in school. While she was by no means fluent, she understood what the man had said. He was pointing out the fact that she was much older than her cousin. Well, he could snicker if he wanted. Ten years wasn't *that* much.

"Thank you," she said, pressing her lips together as he handed her the ticket without another word.

Then, as they stood awkwardly, she went on. "Would you excuse me? I really need a coffee and perhaps the ladies' washroom." Catching Sarah's eye, she lifted her bag slightly. "Mind watching this?

"Sure." Sarah tilted her head to one side as she glanced back and forth between Julien and Angelina. Shrugging, she moved to sit down. "Our flight doesn't leave for another forty minutes anyway."

"Thanks. I'll be back in fifteen." She dropped her bag at Sarah's feet, slid the ticket into her purse, and bustled away, not looking at Julien or his mother again.

That was intense. She ran fingers through her tangled hair until they stuck, thinking she'd find a bathroom first and take her brush to the knots. Maybe she should refresh her lipstick too and try to get that coffee stain out of her shirt.

Minutes later, she leaned over the sink and examined herself in the mirror. She looked flustered. *Great.* That wasn't the image she'd wanted to present. Her eyes always turned a deep green when she was either angry or upset, and they looked like emeralds right now. Swinging her hair forward, she brushed it with vigour. She would have to control her feelings of dislike for the man. Perhaps he wasn't using her cousin for his own ends. She would have to give him a chance before castigating him for it. At least the mother, Elyse, appeared nice.

She flipped her hair back over her shoulders and

stuffed the brush into her purse. Lipstick, that's what she needed. Reaching back in, she rummaged around until she found it and applied a liberal coat. Then, she surveyed herself once more. Better. Smooshing her lips together, Angelina wet a scrap of paper towel and dabbed at her shirt. The brown paper disintegrated and made a worse mess than what had been there to begin with. She grimaced and tossed it away.

Emerging from the bathroom, she spotted a familiar coffee shop and hurried toward it. A nice hot drink would help to calm her nerves. There was a queue, but she didn't think it would take too long to get what her body craved.

Blowing on the coffee as she walked, Angelina took a tiny sip and peered through the steam, searching for the rest of her group where she'd left them.

They were gone. She scanned the waiting area, there was no one. She must have taken longer than she thought. Fishing a hand into her bag she withdrew the ticket and checked the gate number, then the time.

Blast! If she didn't hurry, her bag would take the journey without her. She ran, slopping hot liquid over herself and quickly tossed it into a bin. So much for that idea. Thankfully, Sarah and her friends had been sitting not too far from the gate. Shaking the coffee off her hand, Angelina drew out her passport and ticket. The flight attendant was issuing a final boarding call as she dashed up, panting, and thrust her papers at the woman just as the announcement ended.

"*Bonjour madam.*" With tightened features, the attendant glanced at her, checking that the passport photo matched the face of Angelina Fisk. Satisfied, the woman handed it back and motioned with a wave that she should hurry. The plane must have been waiting for her. She ran.

With her purse banging against her hip, Angelina dashed down the jet bridge and rounded a bend. The plane door was open ahead and two flight attendants waited for her, one looking meaningfully at his watch.

"I'm so sorry," she gasped, producing her documents again. The other man nodded, looking less concerned about her tardiness.

He took her ticket and stepping back with an appreciative grin, directed her to the far side of the plane. "Seat 5D, *mademoiselle*."

Thanking him, she rushed around the corner. Wow. Her fingers flew up to cover her open mouth. She just realised what it meant to have a ticket purchased for her by someone with wealth at their fingertips. A first class seat was exciting. Whenever she'd flown before, she was crammed into economy, stuck between people who either slept on her shoulder or snored in her ear. This was going to be amazing. It was a kind thing for him to have done. Though the only downside was that she now felt indebted to the man, Julien.

Sarah waved to her from the righthand space of the two middle seats on the plane. Julien was on Angelina's side, already staring out his window with seeming disinterest. His mother, Elyse, was on the far side, closer to Sarah.

"I brought your backpack onboard with my own carryon, Cuz," Sarah exclaimed. Her eyes glowed with pleasure. "Come sit down."

Without observing her surroundings to any degree,

Angelina scurried along the aisle toward her cousin, conscious of having held everyone up with her late arrival. Still, she thought she'd take another moment to thank Julien again. Because of that, she failed to notice the long strap of someone's purse that had fallen in front of her. Catching a toe of her high sandals in the belt, she stumbled, her arms flew out, and a screech left her lips. However, she was beyond the seatbacks she grappled for, and her feet went out from under her. She sprawled into Julien's lap, flinging herself over him like a wet blanket.

"Oh!" she spluttered, struggling to remove herself from his body without actually touching him. "I'm so terribly sorry."

He chuckled in her ear, which only increased the hot flush she knew covered her face. His hands slid around her waist, helping to push her onto her feet as she flailed arms and legs in an effort to stand.

"Please, Mademoiselle Fisk. We 'ave only just met," he said, laughing outright now.

"Angelina," she corrected sarcastically, not daring to look at him. What an irritating man. She pulled her purse back into place and tucked her hair behind her ears only to have it slide forward to cover her face. Maybe that was for the best, since her cheeks were flaming red.

"I—I wanted to thank you again for the ticket. I've never had such a pampered seat before." She attempted to push her hair out of the way once more. "I didn't mean to topple on you like a felled tree."

Still grinning, Julien lifted a muscular shoulder and shook his head in a way that said it was nothing. "*Mais,* you are welcome. 'Owever, your method of showing appreciation is most unusual. I 'ave to say I like it."

Ugh! He was laughing at her expense for the second time in one bloody hour. And why was he flirting with her when he'd invited Sarah to stay at his villa, or chateau, or whatever the heck it was?

"Yes, well, I just wanted to tell you. And, as you already know, *Julien*, that fall was an accident." She emphasized his name with a disdainful drawl, and her blood boiled as she heard him chuckle again.

Turning away, she caught sight of Sarah's face. The young woman looked furious. Leaving Julien to buckle himself in, Angelina stepped across the aisle on unsteady limbs and dropped into her seat. She waved at Elyse, who was speaking to a flight attendant, reached across the low divider for her cousin's hand, and pasted a false brightness on her face.

"Made it. Sorry I took so long, Sarah. Thanks for bringing my bag." The young woman avoided Angelina's gesture and began to fuss with her cell phone.

"No problem," she said, a cool edge to Sarah's voice as she continued to look down. Angelina held back a frustrated sound, grateful that Julien and his mother were far enough away that they couldn't hear her response to Sarah's petulance.

"Look, I'm not interested in Julien," Angelina raised herself up to lean closer and whisper. "I genuinely tripped. I don't even like the man, okay?"

"Really?" Sarah's blue eyes met Angelina's and her mouth curled into a grin. "You don't?"

"Really." Angelina settled back in her seat and unslung her purse to find her own phone. "Let's just relax and enjoy this comfort, shall we? I know I'll never have it again." As Sarah agreed and reached out to turn on the TV screen in front of her, Angelina tapped a text message to Marcie.

We're on the plane now. Will write you when we arrive in France. I'm glad I came. This guy seems like a jerk. Don't worry, I'll take care of Sarah.

Placing her phone on airplane mode, she slipped it back into her purse, and reached for her seatbelt. Coping with Sarah and her attraction to Julien was going to be a trial, but she hadn't come along thinking it would be a piece of *gateau*. The French word for cake had slipped, unbidden, into her mind. Thank goodness she had some knowledge of the language.

She settled back into her roomy space with a sigh of enjoyment. She didn't have to worry about future difficulties for the next seven hours and she planned to take it easy. This was going to be the best flight she'd ever have.

CHAPTER 3

The movie Angelina had been watching paused as the captain's voice boomed over the speaker to announce they would be landing at Marseille Provence Airport in ten minutes. After having changed planes at Charles de Gaulle Airport, outside Paris, it was exciting for Angelina to think she would soon set foot on French soil. Ever since taking the language as a subject in school, she'd had a desire to see it, especially Provence.

This plane was much smaller than the last, but she still sat against an aisle, since there were only two seats on either side. Sarah had claimed the window for the view, but then closed the shutter and fell asleep. Angelina was across from Julien, same as before, although this time his mother was beside him in the window seat and they spoke quietly together in French.

Angelina checked that her phone and earbuds were back in her purse and her passport was safe. Her stomach flipped with excitement as her eyes drifted to the snippet of blue sky she could see outside the window past Elyse. It had been a long flight, but *très confortable*. Thanks to the larger space, she'd had some sleep and felt refreshed and alert.

She giggled to herself. Whenever French words popped into her head it took her back to all the dreams she'd had as a teenage girl. Visions of living in France one day, of becoming a writer, and perhaps meeting a handsome countryman with whom to share her life.

She gave herself a shake. *Forget that!* Her gaze had shifted across to Monsieur Julien Belliveau and that was certainly *not* where she wanted it. The man was, no doubt, a lecherous swine. His true character would come to light once she had a chance to see what expectations he had of her cousin, but he would soon learn who he was dealing with. Angelina sighed. She had no business being happy. She was here only to serve a purpose—protect Sarah from the machinations of this man and prevent her from getting hurt.

Angelina grasped her cousin's bare arm to gently shake her. The girl came awake with a start and sat upright.

From across the way, Elyse Belliveau waved. "We 'ave arrived," she called. "I believe it will be a good day." She gestured out the window with her lips stretched over perfect white teeth.

It was the longest sentence the woman had spoken yet. Perhaps she knew more English than had first appeared. It had been weighing on Angelina's mind that she'd have to translate everything that the lady said, and she wondered how Sarah had become so close to the pair in Quebec if the three of them hadn't been able to converse.

Both Sarah and Angelina spoke cheery greetings in response and then Sarah leaned across Angelina's lap and spoke to Julien.

"*Bonsoir, mon cher,*" she trilled. Angelina shrank back into her seat, her insides clenching. She ventured a glance at Julien and thought she saw his lips compress before he composed a tight smile. Was he displeased with the endearment for some reason? She knew she was.

"I think you mean, *bonjour,*" he said, inclining his head toward them. "*Bonsoir* means good evening, and it is early afternoon, *n'est-ce pas*? I 'ope you slept well."

Sarah nodded, looking a bit flustered. Angelina considered the fact that he had corrected Sarah on using the wrong greeting, but hadn't said a word about the fact that she had just called him 'her darling'.

Further discussion was prevented by a final pass of the flight attendants and moments later they were landing. As the plane skidded onto the tarmac, a thrill went up Angelina's spine. She was really here. She would have liked to peer out the window, but she would see the landscape soon enough. Tapping her fingers on the armrest, Angelina waited while they taxied to the terminal and stopped.

As usual, everyone leaped to their feet and began to rummage for belongings, even though the doors wouldn't be opened for at least five to ten minutes. It would be refreshing to be one of the first people to leave and not have anyone jostle or elbow her as she stood. *How nice it must be to be wealthy*, she thought.

Beside her, Julien rose, stretched, and then opened the bin over his head to retrieve his luggage.

Right! She'd thrown her backpack up there when they changed planes in Paris. She clicked open the storage container above her head, but it was empty. Strange. Standing on tiptoes she caught sight of it at the very back of the compartment. Her luggage was so small that it had slid almost out of view.

Meanwhile, she felt movement at her back and squealed as she turned and bumped into Julien's arm.

"Do not worry," he said. "I'm not about to jump on you as you seem so fond of doing to others. I am simply 'anding you your..." he reached past her, dragged her backpack forth and hung the old blue bag from his fingers, "*valise*."

Her face suffused with colour again. He was mocking her bag. Granted, it was old and everyone else had slick, hard-shell, rolling suitcases. But she didn't travel often and wasn't flush with money like some people. There was no need for her to have an up-to-date *valise*, as he had called it.

"Thank you," she said, stiffening her back and lifting her chin. "I prefer to travel light." Meanwhile, Julien lowered Sarah's case to the floor and extended the handle to pull along with his own. He insisted on carrying it for the young woman.

"*Merci*," Sarah called, accepting his help with a flutter of her long lashes. She slung a voluminous purse over her shoulder and stared at Julien with open admiration.

Shifting her backpack to her right hand, Angelina struggled to pull the straps over her shoulders, but they caught on the light jacket she'd worn for the trip and stuck. She could have hit something in frustration at this point. Knowing it was inevitable, she sagged with resignation as Julien's fingers extricated the bands and helped to settle the heavy sack into place.

"I appreciate your assistance," she said. Twisting about, she looked at him with what she hoped was cool disdain. His face was impassive, but there was the tiniest glimmer of laughter in his eyes. Blast the man!

Purposely, she turned her back on him and spoke to her cousin.

"Got everything?" It was an unnecessary question, but it helped to refocus her thoughts. She also hoped that Sarah hadn't witnessed the exchange she'd had with Julien or there would be more jealousy to cope with. *This really wasn't going to be easy.*

The attendant beckoned to them from the front of the plane. With relief, she followed the lady ahead of her as they made their way out. Really, it might not be the easiest of situations to deal with, but she was in France thanks to Sarah and this enigmatic man, Julien. As well as due to the strange series of events that had transpired in the past few days. How quickly things could change in life.

Once clear of the passenger boarding bridge, the group of four gathered into a little huddle. Sarah squeezed Angelina's hand as Julien Belliveau returned Sarah's luggage and issued instructions on navigating the airport.

"We 'ave a car outside in the parking lot," he explained. "You will go through customs and the officer will want to know where you are staying. This will take you longer than us. Do you 'ave the address Sarah?" She nodded. "*Bien.* After you gather your luggage downstairs, we will be out front with the car. It is a black Lexus. *D'accord?*"

"Yes, thank you. That's great," Angelina answered for them both. Sarah's head was tilted to one side and her lips were parted in subconscious adoration of the man. Angelina wanted to shake the girl. Instead, she took her by the arm and propelled her along the passageway with the other tourists who hurried toward customs, passports in hand.

"I know you like him. But you've got to get a grip on yourself." Angelina drew a long breath and looked sideways at her cousin.

"I don't just *like* Julien," Sarah said, closing her eyes and lifting her face to the sunlight that streamed through the long airport windows. "I *love* him."

"Good grief," Angelina muttered. She didn't feel this was the right time for a chat concerning true love. "Come on, let's get in line."

They shuffled down the corridor with countless chattering visitors to France. The lines were long. Eventually, they took their turn at the kiosk, answered several questions about their stay, and their passports were given the stamp of approval.

"Look," Sarah said, holding her passport up to admire. "My very first European stamp. I wonder how things will change when I'm Mrs. Sarah Belliveau? Will I have two passports? I'd become a French citizen, right?"

"I suppose you would, in time." Angelina had only been in France ten minutes and Sarah was already driving her crazy. "However, we don't have time now to discuss the rules of foreign citizenship. We need to follow the signs to pick up your bags. I'm sure you brought more than your carry-on?"

"Of course." Sarah tossed her head. "I have a man to catch and brought a wardrobe to do it. What about you?" She eyed Angelina's stuffed backpack with revulsion. "You have more than just that dingy old thing, right?"

"No," Angelina bit off the word and pushed through a throng of people who were blocking the aisle to talk, leaving Sarah a few paces behind. She wasn't about to discuss her lack of appropriate clothing with a besotted girl that was so bent on capturing a man she could think of nothing else.

And, in truth, Angelina didn't have a lot of up-to-date outfits or dresses. Work had consumed most of her time for the past three years with early mornings, late days, and occasional breakdowns that kept her away from home. Then, after becoming a trusted member of the gravel hauling company, she had even less time when she was asked to train new drivers.

Even her relationship with Bryan had been low-key. Looking back on it she realised they'd never really gone anywhere. His work had taken him out of town a lot and when they were together, they mostly stayed at her apartment. It was clear to her now, she hadn't meant much more to him than a stopover. How gullible she'd been. Sighing, she cast her thoughts back to the night Marcie and Alec had gathered the family to hear the big news.

Once Angelina decided to go, Marcie had made a quick call to Sarah. She'd let her know the change in plans, so that the name could be changed on the ticket.

Then she'd stayed overnight at Angelina's apartment to help pack. After they'd examined her closet, Marcie had flopped onto the bed and flung her arms over her head in despair.

"You have a few cute things, but you can't go to France with ripped jeans and old t-shirts. I mean, they aren't even nice, ripped jeans. They're ripped, because they're old and you snagged them on a fence or something!" Marcie had been exasperated.

But there hadn't been time to go shopping. Somehow, they'd assembled a passible wardrobe for Angelina to take along. Besides, it wasn't necessary that she look super attractive, anyhow, she'd told her sister. She had no one to impress.

Hitching her bag higher up on her back, she forced her thoughts to the present and lengthened her stride. There would be no more stumbling around for her. Somewhere in the distance, she could hear the clickety-click of Sarah's spike heels as she strove to keep up. Angelina's heart relented.

"Sorry Sarah. I'll slow down." She stopped and waited. "Look, there's an elevator ahead. I think we should take it and save your feet some punishment."

Sarah agreed with a brief smile.

Nothing more was said until they passed through the wide revolving door of the exit and reached the sidewalk outside. It was like walking into an oven. Angelina had known it would be hot in the south of France, in late July, but even a sweltering day in Canada wouldn't feel this overwhelming.

Sarah stood her carry-on upright and shaded her eyes against the sun as she perused the oncoming traffic. Angelina did the same with Sarah's oversize, black suitcase, and stood beside her cousin. The bag felt as though it had been packed with rocks. It had been tricky to swing the thing down off the carrousel, but Angelina had managed it. Feeling perspiration break out, she tore off the jacket she'd been wearing and tied it around one of the handles.

"I think I see him," Sarah said. She flapped her arm wildly and Angelina squinted at the many cars, taxis, and buses that were pushing through the area. At length, one vehicle disentangled itself from the throng.

The sleek black car purred up beside them and stopped. Julien stepped out and hurried around the front to take the bags from their hands. His eyebrows lifted as he took in Sarah's matching set of massive luggage, next to Angelina's small backpack. He set them all in the trunk with the same attention given to each item, and then ushered the two women into the back seat. Sliding behind the wheel, Julien checked his mirrors and smoothly edged into traffic.

"I hope you both enjoy your stay with us," said Elyse. Both Angelina and Sarah leaned forward to assure her that they would. The woman's English seemed not bad at all.

Sarah rested a hand on Julien's shoulder to chat as they motored past the soaring windows of the terminal and onto a busy highway. Angelina sank into the luxurious upholstery of the car and allowed her eyes to drift. Granted, they were still travelling in an urban area filled with businesses and rows of red-roofed houses backing up to craggy looking hills, but she was in France, and to her, it was all beautiful.

Angelina consulted her phone and realised it had adjusted to European time. Two o'clock in the afternoon. Hastily, she remembered to send a quick text to Marcie, letting her know they'd arrived, and all was well. Then, tossing her phone back into her purse, she let it drop to the floor unheeded.

Craning her head to look up, she found there wasn't a cloud in the sky. Light flooded the world, leaving shade at a premium. It wasn't surprising she didn't see anyone walking at this time of day. It was too hot.

Trees of varying shapes and sizes whipped by. She'd read about plane trees, sycamore, and cypress, and could see them in the distance. Only, what drew her attention were the tiny plots featuring olive trees, seemingly in people's backyards. At least, she thought that's what they were. Silvery, delicate-looking leaves rippled in the sunshine over squat gnarled trunks.

Not far away to her left, water sparkled. She wondered what it was. Surely not the Mediterranean? It didn't look *azure* enough. Angelina smiled to herself.

"There is not much to see yet," Julien spoke loudly, breaking into her thoughts. Angelina jumped. He must have noticed that she was interested in viewing the landscape flying by the window rather than listening to their conversation. Sarah stopped talking and slid back in her seat to cross her arms.

"The airport is about twenty-seven kilometres northwest of Marseille, but as we drive further north it is still a busy area. It will be a few more minutes before we are in open country." Julien waved a hand to illustrate his remark. "In case you wondered, the water on your left is *Étang de Berre*. It is a lagoon; linked to the

Mediterranean by canals, but it is not the Mediterranean." He grinned into the mirror, as though he had been reading her mind.

Elyse cleared her throat with a small cough before joining in.

"My family has lived in the department of the *Bouches-du-Rhône*, for more than three-hundred-twenty years," she added, with a wide sweep of her tailored arm. "The chateau itself was built in the 1700s. Our vineyards and olive groves lie in the shadow of *le Lançon-Provence* hills and cover seventy-five hectares of *le meilleur terroir*." She spoke distinctly, as though every word had been cut from a visitor's guide to the area and pasted onto her lips.

"Does terroir mean the soil?" Sarah asked, sliding forward again.

"*Oui.*" Elyse moved in another expressive shrug. "It refers to the many things that make up a location used for growing—the soil, the climate, the environment unique to a certain area, even the type of farming practise. *Le terroir* is many things, but all of them contribute to the character of the wine or the olive oil produced."

"Interesting," Sarah exclaimed. She faced Angelina and spoke with feeling. "Julien and Elyse have a beautiful home. Wait till you see it." Julien glanced back at Sarah, and she coloured. "At least, from the pictures you showed me it looked beautiful."

"It is," Julien agreed, smiling at her, his eyes crinkling with good humour. "*Le château est très beau.*"

Silence fell in the vehicle, yet it was companionable. Both Sarah and Angelina settled back in their seats to gaze out the windows.

Finally, they broke free of the sprawling city limits of Marseille. Long, spiky grass twirled in the wind of their passing at the edge of the paved road, most of it browned from heat and lack of water. Farms and fields began to appear; the soil, a light sandy colour, laced with small rocks. Rows upon rows of vines fanned out from the confines of these fields and stretched into the distance. Areas of the same pale-green, feathery-looking trees marched solidly down other plots of land.

After only about fifteen minutes of driving, they entered a roundabout and exited onto a narrower road, heading west. Olive groves grew in abundance here. Angelina marvelled at the chalky blocks of limestone thrusting from the earth to create a ragged edge against the sky.

Sooner than expected, the car slowed, and Julien signaled to the right. A large sign announced the family name Belliveau, hours of operation, and other information, but they swept past it too fast for her to read. Angelina stared as the car curved onto a paved driveway lined with cypress and continued toward brick buildings that hunched in the shadow of the limestone hills. They passed a large parking lot on the left where further signage encouraged visitors to take guided tours of the olive groves and vineyards.

Even the parking lot was pretty, she reflected. It was bordered all around with a low stone fence, and a hedge of lavender had been established beside the wall, running the entire distance. Although it was likely too late in the year to see the aromatic plant in full bloom, a few purple sprigs of lavender still poked higher than the rest.

A building, its front covered with vines, stood at one end, clearly open to the public. Angelina supposed it was a shop where the produce of the estate was sold. The area was busy with people making their way either back to their cars, their arms laden with bags and bottles, or walking into the sanctuary of the shaded building. Many more structures, all built of the same light-coloured stone, were scattered about, as well as large cylindrical tanks behind a chain-link fence.

They kept driving. Still obscured from view by the tall pine trees that surrounded it, the chateau was like a hidden treasure. Finally, Julien maneuvered the car around a bend and up a steep slope where the house appeared, magnificent before them. Angelina sucked in a breath. It was huge. This square, two-storied building with large round turrets on every end, resembled a fairy-tale palace more than a house. Was this really where Julien and his mother lived?

Despite its size, the chateau looked loved. There was a warmth to the honey-coloured stone and thick, red, clay-tiled roof. All along the front, beneath the many recessed windows, was a profusion of peonies ranging from white, pink, and red all the way to yellow. Vines crept their way across the stones and hung low overtop the polished wooden doors of the entry.

"Oh wow," Sarah moaned softly. Angelina flicked her a glance. Hopefully, the young woman wouldn't say something inappropriate about hoping to become mistress of the place. But Angelina forgot her concerns as they stopped before a broad flight of stairs, also cut from stone. Julien turned off the motor.

"*Voila*," he said. Getting out of the car, he opened

Sarah's door and bowed with a flourish. "Welcome to the home and estate of my forefathers—Chateau de Belliveau."

He could hardly be blamed for indulging in a little pomp and ceremony, Angelina thought as she opened her door and slid out of the car with purse in hand. Pushing a cloud of dark hair from her eyes, she moved to the back of the car and waited for him to open the trunk. Elyse stayed where she was until her son opened the door and helped her to rise.

"Thank you, I'll take my own," Angelina said, as he grabbed her backpack first and made to sling it over his arm. His eyes met hers in a brief, freezing moment.

"Are you a feminist, Miss—Angelina?" Julien asked. One by one he lifted the cases from the spacious trunk of the car and set them on the pavement, then stood with hands on hips awaiting her answer. Sarah and Elyse went quiet.

"I would not classify myself as a feminist, no." She shifted her purse to rest against her hip. "I appreciate it when a man opens a door, gives me his seat, or shows me some small courtesy, but I also believe in equality. If I do the same job as a man, I expect to be paid the same amount."

"And you would want to be considered a man in *all* respects?" Julien appeared to be deliberately provoking her. He motioned that she precede him up the stairs with his mother and Sarah. A member of their staff threw open the double doors above them and hurried down the steps to relieve Julien of half the cases.

"*Salut*, Louis," said Elyse, catching the man's arm as

he hurried past. *"Tu vas bien?"* The man patted her hand and grinned.

"Oui, merci," he said, reaching for Sarah's large cases.

"You're mincing words," Angelina called over her shoulder. Taking care, lest she make another foolish move and tumble to Julien's feet, she marched up the staircase behind her cousin.

"It may surprise you to know I haven't spent my formative years embroidering pillow shams or arranging flowers for a drawing room." She forced herself to remain calm. "I've worked hard to be taken seriously in a field of employment that's almost exclusively made up of men. When I was treated the same as any member of that team, even if it meant I was to receive criticism or correction, I was glad. As long as the issue was truly my mistake," she hastened to clarify. "And so, if you think that means I wish to be treated like a man, then yes, I guess I do."

As she spoke, her irritation grew with the man. He was arrogant; taking some sadistic pleasure in toying with her, she was sure of it.

"Bravo!" Elyse halted in the doorway ahead of her and beamed at Angelina. "Do you find fault with this way of thinking, Julien? Because I believe it to make perfect sense." Elyse watched her son ascend the steps with luggage in tow.

"So do I," interjected Sarah, not to be left out of any discussion involving Julien. The man carrying Sarah's things disappeared within the house, but the four of them stopped on the broad expanse of stone before the door.

"Naturally, it makes sense." Julien smiled at his

mother as he set the cases down and stood beside Angelina. "I was merely asking for interest's sake. She is correct on all counts, and I'm sure is accomplished in this male-dominated workplace she speaks of, whatever it is." Lowering his voice for her ears only, he added, "And if she is perhaps a little unsteady on her feet I'm sure they are forgiving." Angelina flashed him a look of annoyance and sniffed. He just had to have the last word.

Julien caught her malevolent eye. "*Both* of you are the epitome of strong, modern young women," he said, striding through a broad hall whose focal point was a curving white staircase. "Now, shall I show you to your rooms? It has been a long flight and we are all suffering from jetlag."

"Yes please. I mean, *s'il vous plaît*," said Sarah, with a flat English accent. She flashed her hosts a row of white teeth and freshly applied pink lipstick as she clicked across the terracotta tiles in her high heels.

Julien turned to wink at her in approval before continuing to lead the way to the sweeping staircase. "*Tres bien*, Sarah."

Angelina admired the blue and white floor as they passed through. Every second tile was imprinted with a blue *Fleur-de-lis* which was a lovely accent to the impressive chamber they walked through. She followed the group as they climbed the gently curving staircase and stopped on the thick carpet of the landing.

"*Merci* Louis," Julien thanked the man who had carried Sarah's things. "You may leave the cases here." The fellow nodded without meeting any of their eyes, bustled back downstairs, and out of sight.

"Excuse me while I see my mother to her apartment." Julien spoke with formality. "It will only take a moment."

Before Elyse turned to follow her son, the lady looked at each of them, her eyes crinkling with warmth and welcome.

"We shall meet downstairs in the dining room for dinner in one hour. That is early, by our standards, but I think we could all do with some refreshment. Can you be ready, or would you prefer to have a nap?"

"I won't need a nap." Sarah reached for her case and snapped up the handle. "I'll just freshen up and be ready at..." she consulted her smartwatch, "five-thirty?"

"Perfect," Elyse said. "Follow the hallway to the left when you arrive downstairs in the foyer. We will meet you there."

Angelina stared around her as they waited for Julien to return. The enormous hallway was bright with light from floor-to-ceiling latticed windows behind her and similar ones a distance away on the other side of the stairwell. They were draped with a soft, filmy lace in the palest sea green that moved in a breeze. Down the hall, she could see doors leading to rooms on either side, and in both directions.

Dangling over the top of the stairwell was the largest chandelier Angelina had ever gazed upon. Tiny rainbows of light danced around her on the ivory-coloured walls. Mesmerized, she turned full circle to enjoy them and saw Sarah preening herself in the golden light of a gilt-framed mirror.

A door closed at the far end of the hall and footsteps could be heard from around the corner where Julien and his mother had disappeared. With one last fluff of her hair, Sarah moved to lean artfully against the banister. Her blonde hair shimmered in the late afternoon sun and her figure was flawless.

She instinctively appeared to know how best to pose or which way to turn in the light to look her best in every situation. Angelina was impressed with her cousin's attention to detail. She was determined to succeed in capturing this man. True, Angelina also took pains with her own appearance, but then she promptly forgot about it. This girl had effortless beauty down to a science.

Angelina watched Julien walk toward them with a fluid grace and almost regal bearing. *He could easily pass for the king of this castle, and he certainly acted like it.* Shaking herself, she pasted a brightness on her face she didn't feel and put a thumb under her backpack in readiness. She understood that he couldn't help but notice the younger woman. His eyes flicked toward Sarah with appreciation, and he laughed as, clinging to the rail, she leaned into his path.

"What a fabulous house you have Julien. Thank you so much for inviting me." Giggling, she spun around to lay a pink-tipped hand on his sleeve. He stopped to cover it with one of his own. She flashed a look at Angelina and the happiness left her face. "I mean, for inviting *us*."

"You are entirely welcome," he said. "Both of you. However, if you will follow me, ladies," he said, stooping to extend the handle of the heaviest of Sarah's cases and drag it in the opposite direction. "Your rooms are this way."

Groaning under her breath, Angelina trailed after the good-looking pair in front of her. She knew Sarah's feelings for him were nothing more than infatuation, but she couldn't be sure about Julien. If he was out to use her cousin and leave her sobbing by the edge of a road, he'd have trouble on his hands.

CHAPTER 4

Angelina bumped her backpack into the door as she leaned against it to stare at the room she'd been given. It was one of the turrets. If she were to have assembled the space herself, she could not have chosen anything more beautiful.

The bedroom wasn't large by the standards of French aristocracy, but it was perfect for her. The walls were painted a similar sea green colour to the curtains down the hall, and two sets of white, latticed windows opened onto a beautiful world of rolling hills, vineyards, and olive groves beyond.

Beneath one set of windows a wide seat had been constructed, and cushions matching the heavy brocade curtains that hung above it were arranged for the occupant to sit and gaze upon the scenery or read a book of wild fancy. Her eyes fell upon an armoire of a slightly deeper shade that stood solidly in one corner. Its arched doors were covered with spotless mirrored panes that reflected the blue of the sky outside. It wasn't a modern piece of furniture, but had the look of a refurbished antique. Beneath the doors, closer to the floor, were two drawers in which she thought she'd store her folded items. In another corner stood a white desk with a chair in the same style as the headboard of the double bed at the center of the room and the armoire.

The soft bed called to her, but she was too excited to be sleepy. Pulling her backpack off her shoulders, she tossed it to the floor. The coverlet of creamy white was far too nice to throw her old bag upon it. She walked over to the other window in the room, realizing it was more than what she'd first thought. It was one large French door.

"Oh, that's lovely." She pulled the handle and stepped onto a tiny balcony fitted with an ornate bistro table and matching chair. While the other windows looked toward the front of the chateau, this space afforded her a view of the side and back of the house where a manicured garden and pool met up with mountainous terrain and a wild tangle of stunted trees and shrubs.

Angelina was thrilled. Dropping into the chair, she lifted her chin to the heat of the sun and drank it in. She envisioned herself relaxing out here in the cool evening with a glass of wine and the book she'd brought.

A sound caught her attention. Standing, she leaned on the railing and peered below to see Julien exit the house in swimming trunks. With a towel around his neck and sandals, he looked like a whole new man. An extremely attractive man, she thought, before blinking rapidly to rid herself of the image and stepping back inside her room. But before she could close the door against his charms, she heard him speak.

"No, I 'ave not told her and I 'ave no intention of doing so," Julien was talking to someone. Angelina leaned back outside the open door and craned her neck to see if he was alone. His deep voice floated up to her once more.

"This is not for you to decide and is certainly none of your business! You will say nothing, or you will 'ave me to deal with," he snapped into a cell phone. With an angry flick of his wrist, he spun the device onto a deckchair, dropped his towel, and dove into the shimmering pool.

Well, that was interesting. Angelina moved back into her room this time and softly closed the door behind her lest he realise she had overheard his rant. She couldn't help but wonder who he had been talking too, and about what. He was upset, that much was obvious, and whoever he'd been speaking to didn't understand French. Her suspicions about him resurfaced. Clearly the man was hiding something, and it sounded serious.

She glanced at her own smartwatch and realised she only had half an hour to prepare for the meal with Sarah and Elyse. She hadn't even had a chance to talk to Sarah alone since the trip began. There were several questions she'd like to ask, such as the whereabouts of Elyse's husband, Julien's father, who the mother and son had been visiting in Canada, and how Sarah had inveigled an invitation to visit them here. She knew so little about these people with whom she was to stay. Her sister

Marcie must have known more, but there had been no time to discuss details of the trip.

She moved to unpack her humble bag and stow her things in the charming armoire. It was surprising how much could be stuffed in a small space with some artful rolling. She unfurled her dresses, one at a time and shook them. They were wrinkled, but perhaps if she took them with her as she showered, the material would relax a little in the steam.

Carrying them to the beautiful old closet, she opened both doors and reached for an armful of hangers. Strange. Inside, there were several men's shirts and a worn leather jacket. They looked too large for Julien. She wondered if they belonged to Elyse's husband or another son. She fingered the soft brown coat and wondered if she should just leave the items or take them to Elyse. She decided she would leave them alone for now and pushed them to one side.

Angelina hung up her tops and all the wrinkled outfits except one deep blue dress that flattered her slim figure, before unpacking the rest of her things. She laid two pairs of jeans in the bottom drawer and her underwear with her pyjamas in the top, smaller drawer. The book she set on the windowsill to read later and then tossed her makeup bag onto the desk in the corner. Done. That hadn't taken long.

Grabbing the dress, she arranged it on a hanger and carried it into the adjoining bathroom. There was no time for a bath, although the tub looked inviting, if you liked lounging in sudsy water. As a rule, Angelina preferred the speed of a shower. Even a tub as large and wide as this one held no appeal for her.

Hanging her clothing behind the door, she clipped up her hair and stepped into the walk-in shower to revel in the feel of warm water coursing down her body.

Minutes later she wrapped a voluminous towel about herself and rubbed away the steam to examine her face in the mirror. After applying mascara to her already thick fringe of lashes, and dabbing some shimmer above her green eyes, she briefly stepped back to examine herself. There wasn't time for fussing. Slipping into her dress and then into the pair of gold, flat sandals she'd managed to squish into her bag, she reached for her purse and withdrew a matching shade of lip-gloss. *It would have to do.* With one last rapturous look around her room, she opened the door and went in search of Sarah.

Angelina knocked on her cousin's door, but there was no answer. Either the girl had gone down without her, or Sarah was resting. Turning, she made her way back along the hall and down the sweeping staircase, all the while trying unsuccessfully to smooth the wrinkles out of her dress with her hands.

A woman, carrying a stack of folded towels, met her as she reached the ground floor. The woman beckoned to Angelina with a free hand.

"Follow me, *s'il vous plaît?*"

Nodding, Angelina walked across the patterned tiles and through an archway into a spacious dining room. She was sure the table itself would have seated twenty people, and a stone fireplace took up a large part of one whole wall. Fawn-coloured beams lined the ceiling, and another, smaller chandelier hung over the table, adding subtle ambiance and a feeling of ancient grandeur to the room.

Elyse and Sarah were already seated and in deep discussion, but both women looked up as Angelina entered the room.

"Join us, my dear," Elyse said and fluttered a hand toward the chair at her left side. A man bustled through an opening at the far end of the room, carrying a large platter of a colourful salad. Setting it in front of Madame Belliveau with a thump, he hurried away only to return with a bottle of wine before Angelina had crossed the room.

Elyse poured a sparkling measure of the wine into each glass and then lifted hers to join them in a toast. Angelina quickly sat, took one, and together they clinked in unison.

"*À votre santé*." Elyse said, looking at each of the ladies as they tipped their glasses and echoed her words. The cold, sweet liquid ran down Angelina's throat. It was delicious.

"Is this wine what you create here?" she asked, taking another sip.

"*Oui*," the lady said with quiet pride. "We produce wine and olive oil on the estate as my family has done for many years." She set her glass down and looked at each of them in turn. "But we must eat. The chef has prepared *la salade niçoise pour vous*. It is a popular dish in the south of France, although people sometimes argue over the correct ingredients."

"How special," Sarah said, leaning over the dish to examine each element. "I see there are, boiled eggs, tomatoes, green beans, lettuce, and some sort of fish...I think?" She looked questioningly at Elyse.

"*Oui*. It is fresh tuna. The vegetables are grown in our garden and the dressing is prepared with our own olive oil. It is *tres bien*, very good. Please, try it." Urging them to help themselves, she grasped her wine, sat back in her chair, and smiled indulgently as they dug in.

Angelina and Sarah took a mouthful and exchanged wide-eyed looks of enjoyment.

"What a treat this is! *Merci beaucoup*." Angelina raised a quartered tomato on the end of her fork and waved it toward Elyse in appreciation. The lady beamed.

Without warning, a door banged outside and raised voices were heard. Moments later, as Elyse was spooning salad onto her own plate, Julien burst into the room.

"Have you seen the keys to my truck?" he demanded of his mother. His hair was still wet from swimming and standing on end. He had thrown on a t-shirt, but the man still looked devilishly handsome. Angelina glanced at her cousin for a reaction. She understood the fascination Sarah must feel. However, after her own recent experiences, Angelina was content to avoid men for a while.

Elyse leaned back, nonplussed with his loud interruption, and answered him in rapid French. "Work comes later," she concluded in English. She picked up her fork. "Come sit with us now."

"*Desole*," he said, striding toward the table. Angelina couldn't follow what had been said because it was too fast. She only concluded his mother must have reproved him for rude behavior. *Good.*

Dragging out a chair beside Sarah, Julien dropped into it. "I 'ope the rooms are to your liking?"

"Mine's great," Sarah said. She dabbed her mouth with the white linen napkin she'd had on her lap and swivelled to face him. "The view is awesome too. I'd love to see more of the estate when you have time."

Julien nodded as he reached for the salad and pulled a plate toward himself. "*Bien sûr*, of course," he said. "And 'ow about you, Angelina? Are you 'appy with your room?" It took her a moment to answer, as she'd been thinking how beautiful her name sounded when spoken with a French accent. She swallowed hard.

"Yes! It's gorgeous," she answered, blinking. Glancing up, she met his eyes and noticed that he seemed pleased. "I don't think I've ever stayed anywhere so lovely." She looked back down at her salad. She didn't like feeling off-balance around this man or any man. Although she wasn't exactly an extrovert, she was usually quite collected when speaking in awkward situations.

"Wine?" Elyse asked, handing Julien the bottle. Over her shoulder, she called for a staff member to bring more.

"*Merci*," he said. "*Alors*, what would you like to see tomorrow, Sarah?" He forked a mouthful of salad into his mouth and turned his gaze to her cousin. "The vineyard, the olive groves, or the facilities where the magic 'appens." He turned his teasing regard upon her.

Sarah visibly melted. With effort, she dragged

herself back to the meal and managed a bite without taking her eyes off his face.

"I think to walk among the grape vines and olive trees would be divine," she breathed. "Especially in the moonlight."

Angelina averted her eyes lest anyone saw them rolling. All this gushing and simpering was enough to make her physically ill. *And moonlight! Good grief.*

"Sounds good." Angelina interrupted purposely. "I'd like to see that as well." She lifted a few green beans to her mouth and focused on a painting at the far end of the hall. "Although, it might be difficult to walk there at night. Better during daylight hours, don't you agree, Elyse?"

She felt, rather than saw, Sarah's angry glare, but chose to ignore it. Naturally, Sarah was offering herself up on a platter to Julien and he was falling for it. *What guy wouldn't?* Sarah was young, pretty and making herself ridiculously available.

"*Oui, oui*. In fact, I do agree—strongly," Elyse answered with a twinkle in her eye. "A twisted ankle would be most inconvenient for you, *ma chérie.*" The lady rested a small white hand over Sarah's tanned one and patted.

"I suppose you're right." Sarah's shoulders drooped. Pointedly looking across at Angelina, the girl continued. "Whenever you have time to take *me*, Julien, I would love to go."

"*Bien*, it is settled," said Julien, pushing his chair back from the table and picking up his plate. "I believe we should have some coffee on the terrace. As well as something sweet, to finish the meal. Do you agree?"

Sarah twittered again. "I'm sweet," she said, looking up at him with a radiant face. Angelina felt like kicking her cousin under the table as Julien bent over the girl with a wink and added her empty plate to his own.

"You most certainly are, Sarah," he said, moving to stand beside Elyse. "Are you finished *ma mère?*"

In answer, the lady tossed her napkin onto the table. "*Oui. Merci*, Julien."

Before he could ask, or come closer to her, Angelina thrust her plate at him. "It was delicious. Will you tell the cook how much we enjoyed it, please?"

Julien's grey eyes bored into hers as he extended a long arm for her dish. Their fingertips touched and Angelina flinched. She snatched her hand back so fast that she caught the end of her fork and sent it spinning beneath the table with a clatter. To cover her confusion, she dove for it and smashed her head into Julien's, as he did the same.

Straightening, Julien set the dishes on the table while he rubbed his forehead. Angelina flopped back in her chair massaging her own sore spot. She didn't know whether to laugh or apologize—yet again.

"Tell me, *mademoiselle*, are you always this accident prone or 'ave you saved it all for me?" It was a rhetorical question, said Julien retrieved the plates and made his way to the kitchen without waiting for her to respond.

That was just as well, Angelina thought. She had no answer, largely because she didn't know herself. She'd never had so many mishaps before.

Elyse led a glowering Sarah to the terrace with Angelina following behind, feeling somewhat dazed. She rubbed the back of her neck in hopes of relieving the pressure she felt in her muscles and closed her eyes to clear her brain. It was jetlag, she told herself. Things would be better tomorrow after a good sleep.

She yawned just thinking about it. Elyse and Sarah were some distance ahead and she followed them out of the dining room, and onto the terrace Julien had spoken of. Like every other aspect of the house, it was beautiful. Cream paving stones surrounded the sparkling blue pool Angelina had seen from her window, and tables with matching chairs and umbrellas were scattered around the wide area.

Since the sun had partially disappeared behind the chateau, and they now enjoyed some shade, she thought this side of the house must face north.

Ahead of her, Sarah and Elyse had seated themselves on loungers. The older woman rested a hand on the armrest and leaned her glossy head close to catch something Sarah said. She threw back her head and laughed. Angelina relaxed at the sound. Really, Julien could take a few lessons from his mother. She was comfortable to be with, and so welcoming.

Angelina found a chair nearby and settled back, placing her feet upon a stool, and listening to the steady chirrup of—what was that noise. She waited for a lull in their conversation and then asked Elyse.

"The creature that makes that sound is the symbol of Provence." Elyse reclined on the cushions and expelled a long breath before continuing. "They are cicadas; insects similar to locusts I suppose. The males make that sound in order to attract females." She laughed, almost bitterly. "My husband used to joke about it. He said the loudest and most persistent ones get the girls, just like men. Perhaps he was right." Her voice trailed off and she looked up to the rocky hills behind them. She looked sad and Angelina wondered again what had happened to the woman's husband.

At that moment, Julien joined them again. Sarah sat up and clapped her hands with glee as he set down a tray of tiny steaming mugs, glasses with an amber-coloured liquid sloshing to and fro at their bottoms, and a plate of small, iced cakes.

"There is coffee and cognac for each of you, and please, help yourself to the dessert."

Lifting a coffee for himself, he downed it with one gulp, then slipped his hand under the globe of one of the delicate crystal glasses before sitting down.

"*Merci*," Angelina and the two other women chimed together.

"I could not help overhearing you ask about cicadas," he said. "There is a legend told in Provence, that the cicada was sent by God to awaken peasants from their afternoon slumber and thereby avert their lazy ways. The heat," he waved a hand into the air, "can be overwhelming and sometimes puts people to sleep. The story goes on to say that the plan was unsuccessful." Closing his eyes, he leaned back in his own chair.

The group lapsed into silence. There wasn't even a breeze, and the heat was stifling despite the fact the sun was hidden by the house. Angelina flipped the bottom of her dress to create a little wind.

"Your dress is a mass of wrinkles," Sarah said suddenly. "Maybe rolling everything into a dirty old backpack wasn't the best idea."

Angelina knew it was Sarah's age and jealousy talking. But knowing it didn't help to avoid the blush that stole up her neck. She smoothed her hands over the light cotton material.

"After travelling, we all have that difficulty with our clothing," Elyse lowered her cognac and addressed Angelina. "It will be a simple matter to correct. Please give your things to Clarisse, the girl who showed you to the dining room. I will ask her to press them for you."

"I can easily do that myself—" Angelina began, but the lady cut her off with a flourish of her hand.

"*Non*. You are our guest. Please do as I ask...Yes?" Elyse smiled over the rim of her glass.

"Yes," Angelina agreed. "Thank you."

"And what will you do tomorrow, my son?" Elyse turned her attention to Julien.

He opened his eyes a crack. "I'll spend the morning ensuring that the estate has run smoothly in our absence. I 'ope there have been no issues." He swirled the cognac, staring into his glass as though mesmerized. "And then, perhaps the ladies would like to take a guided tour of the facilities before lunch?"

"A tour given by *you*?" Sarah was quick to ask.

"*Bien sûr*, of course with me. After I return from my duties. You don't think I would let two beautiful women wander the grounds alone, do you?" He lifted his glass in a toast and drained the last drop, observing each of them in turn before his eyes rested on Angelina's. "But now, I believe I shall retire to bed. I must be up at five o'clock and I confess to being tired after our trip."

Angelina looked down, feeling flustered again. Blast the man! There was something about those smoky grey eyes of his that caused her stomach to flip. Julien stood and collected their empty glasses.

He paused to place a light kiss on his mother's forehead. "*Bonne nuit*," he said, laying a hand on her shoulder for a moment. Sweeping the tray off the table, he headed back into the house.

Angelina released a breath she didn't know she'd been holding and watched him melt into the shadowy interior. It wasn't late by French time, but for her it was the middle of the night. She could hardly keep her eyes open any longer.

They all rose and exchanged the same French words, wishing each of them a good sleep. She hurried away, glad to escape before Sarah could stop her. Angelina knew instinctively that the girl wanted to warn her away from Julien.

She was interfering with Sarah's plans, and, judging by the looks he was giving her cousin, likely Julien's too. As she climbed the stairs, she recalled the dire warning he had issued on the phone. It sounded ominous. Was it Sarah he'd been talking about?

Re-committing herself to the task at hand, she vowed that nothing would prevent her from protecting her young cousin. Even if it was protecting the girl from herself.

CHAPTER 5

Angelina stretched lazily beneath the light coverings of her bed and squinted at the time on her wrist—eight-thirty. She'd slept longer than she meant to. Although it hadn't been discussed, she didn't think Elyse would be up early, and she felt certain that Sarah wouldn't be either. Thoughts of her cousin had Angelina lunging straight up in bed and resting her head in her hands. Now that they'd both had some rest, she needed to talk to Sarah, alone.

Swinging her legs from under the sheets, she slid to the floor. It was cool and she wriggled her toes on the carpet as she stepped to the windows to draw the curtains and allow light to shine into her room. Then, yawning, she hurried to the bathroom with her towel. Maybe she could catch her cousin before she went down for breakfast. Angelina doubted whether Sarah would come looking for *her* unless it was to tell her to back off. Angelina would have to hurry.

After the shower, and wrapped in the voluminous

white bathrobe, she padded to the window to look out at the new day. It was beautiful here. She pulled open the wide French door and stepped onto her balcony to fling her arms wide, encompassing the world in her happiness.

She leaned on the railing and surveyed all she could see when movement caught her eye. A vehicle pulled up the driveway, stopped by the chateau, and someone got out. Was it—Sarah? Up already and outside? This was not the Sarah she knew and loved. But the girl had said she was here to catch a man. It stood to reason that the other occupant of the vehicle would be Julien and that Sarah had made her move before Angelina was on the scene.

As she watched, the vehicle pulled away and Sarah sashayed down a path toward the house. She wore a wide-brimmed sunhat and sizeable sunglasses. The rest of her was clothed in a hot pink tank top and short shorts, and she hummed to herself as she bent to trail her fingers through lavender growing along the path. Before Angelina could call out to Sarah, asking her to come up for a visit, there was a light tap at her door. She left the window and sprinted across the room.

"Who is it?" she called, leaning her head close to the door.

"Clarisse. I 'ave brought you your clothes."

The night before, after Angelina had been in her room only minutes, Clarisse had knocked and bustled away with all the clothing that needed to be pressed.

Angelina ushered the girl inside. "*Merci beaucoup*," she said. Hurrying to the wardrobe, she pulled both doors wide open. The girl seemed hesitant, so Angelina beckoned to her again. "Let's hang them up right away."

"Oh!" The maid's forward movement froze as she looked into the wardrobe with wide, disbelieving eyes. *"Ces vêtements appartiennent à Monsieur Belliveau,"* she said. Then, remembering she should be speaking in English, she continued in a subdued voice. "This clothing should not be 'ere. It belonged to Georges Belliveau."

"I wondered whose they were, but didn't know what to do with them." Angelina leaned in and slid the leather jacket and shirts from the rail. "Would you please take them to Mrs. Belliveau?"

Angelina laid them carefully on the bed and turned. Clarisse was still staring at the few garments as though they were a nest of rattlesnakes. Only after Angelina held her arms out to the girl and cleared her throat did Clarisse hand over the clothes she'd pressed.

Together they hung Angelina's items inside the armoire, and she grinned her appreciation at the maid to put her at ease. Standing back, Angelina studied the closet, wishing she had a few more outfits. The wardrobe looked empty. *But no use in wishing for something that didn't exist*, she thought, closing the doors.

"Thank you Clarisse, my clothes look so much better now."

Angelina moved to the things lying across her bed. *I should have taken them to Elyse when I first arrived.* Scooping them up and stepping forward she deposited them into Clarisse's waiting arms, noting that the maid did not look happy with the arrangement.

However, the young woman bobbed her head and

scurried away. It was only as the door closed behind her that Angelina noticed something had fallen to the floor. She picked it up, turning it over in her hand. It was a business size envelope, addressed to, '*Monsieur Georges Belliveau.*' The seal had been torn open. She would give it to Elyse.

Already feeling the heat of the sun as it streamed through the large French door, Angelina knew it would be another hot day. She decided to put on her favourite periwinkle-blue, spaghetti-strap dress, add a little makeup, some sunscreen, and find Sarah. After she was dressed, she popped the envelope into one of the embellished front pockets and left the turret.

꙳

IT WASN'T DIFFICULT TO LOCATE THE GIRL. PEALS OF laughter ricocheted around the hall as soon as Angelina stepped off the staircase. Hurrying, she followed the sound, and walked through the dining room and onto the terrace once more. Sarah was stretched across the same lounger, close to the pool in the hot pink outfit Angelina had seen her wearing for her early morning excursion. The tank top was so brief it barely covered her chest. Elyse sat at a nearby table in the shade, sipping a coffee. The aroma was wonderful.

"*Bonjour*, Angelina!" Sarah reared upright, looking joyful. "I was right wasn't I? It's beautiful here." Angelina was pleasantly surprised. Sarah appeared willing to be friends again.

"You were *absolutely* right." Angelina laughed as she took the chair opposite to Elyse and caught her eye.

"It's so kind of you to have us as your guests." She waved an encompassing hand.

"You 'ave never been to France before?"

"No." Angelina moved her chair into the shade beside Elyse. I've been on a few trips to warm countries simply because living in Canada is no picnic in the winter. People often head to a hot destination to break it up." She paused and looked around at her surroundings. "But I've never been to Europe and have always wanted to come to France. Provence in particular. I'm grateful to you that I could."

Elyse looked puzzled. "*Un pique-nique?* In winter?"

Sarah tittered. "She means that winter isn't easy in Canada, not that we have picnics in December. It's too cold."

"Ahh," the lady nodded with a smile. "I understand. It is a saying you 'ave." She placed a delicate hand over her heart. "I am so very pleased to hear you like it in Provence. And Sarah feels the same way, I am sure." She nodded. "But I am forgetting *le petit déjeuner.*" Scraping her chair back, their host stood to her feet. "Excuse me. I shall see about breakfast."

"Oh! Elyse, wait." Angelina suddenly recalled the envelope. She drew it from her pocket and leaned across the table to hand it to the lady. "There were some men's clothes in the armoire of my bedroom. I gave them to Clarisse to bring to you, but this fell out and I didn't notice until she had left."

With trembling fingers Elyse took the envelope and read the inscription. Her breath caught in a sob and turning without a word she hurried away.

"I'll come help you." Sarah called, hopping up. She

seemed to have missed the exchange between Angelina and Madame Belliveau. Though before she darted after Elyse, she stopped beside Angelina and leaned down to give her cousin a hug. "Sorry I was crabby last night," she whispered. "Must have been a lack of sleep." Straightening, she adjusted her sunhat and laughed.

"I've already been off with Julien to see part of the winery. He's such a sweet man, he said he didn't mind taking me with him to check on his business one bit. I mean, I should learn how things run around here." She shooed a bee away from the bright pink flowers on her top.

"Anyway," she looked at the door where Elyse had disappeared, "I want to help Elyse. She's a sweetheart too—in a different way." Chuckling, Sarah jogged to the doorway and ducked inside.

Angelina shook her head, laughing. Sarah was a sweet girl. Impetuous, headstrong, a total flirt and reckless at times, but a sweet girl, nonetheless. She folded her hands over the skirt of her sundress, leaned her head back on the chair and closed her eyes.

"It's nice to see you so relaxed," said a voice.

"Oh!" she came alive with a start, her heart racing. "I didn't hear you arrive."

"I like to sneak up on my victims," Julien said, dropping into the chair next to her with a straight face.

Victims? Was that supposed to mean something? She stared at him with widening eyes.

"It is a joke, *vous comprenez?*" He stared back at her unmoving features for a moment and then pulled his chair a little closer.

"I am sorry I 'ave done something to displease you."

He frowned. "I suppose it was because I teased you on the plane. It was not my intention to anger you, but you 'ave to admit you did throw yourself at me, *n'est-ce pas?*" He raised his eyebrows questioningly as an answering smile lifted the corners of her mouth.

"Please, may we start over? To make peace, for Sarah's sake if nothing more?" He gazed at her with mock pleading, leaning in to watch her face. She looked into the grey eyes that were much closer than what felt comfortable, yet she found it impossible to look away. Her heart raced in response.

Angelina took a steadying breath, raised her hands, and ducked her head in mock defeat. "I give in. You're right. We did get off on the wrong foot. I'd be glad to start over." Clasping her hands together she ventured another look at his face. He was close enough that she could almost feel his breath.

"The wrong—foot?" he repeated, squinting at her with a teasing look on his face again. "Are you referring to your feet and 'ow you have a problem staying on them?"

Glad for his joke that caused her to laugh and break her stupor, Angelina protested. "Okay, you got me."

At that moment, Elyse and Sarah came through the door bearing trays of food and drinks. Julien jumped up, moved his chair back to its original spot and hastened to help his mother. Angelina mentally gave her head a shake and schooled her features back to normal.

Sarah set her tray on the table with a thump and began to unload it. It was a delicious breakfast of fresh fruit, flakey croissants, strawberry preserves, and coffee.

She handed Angelina a plate and popped several grapes into her mouth before seating herself.

"Julien says we could walk through the olive groves this morning, while the sun isn't so hot," she said, chewing. "That okay with you Angelina?" Without waiting for an answer, she went on. "Can I pour everyone some coffee?"

The atmosphere was less tense now, after Julien and Angelina had put their differences behind them. She watched him from beneath her lashes. He seemed nice enough and she supposed he and Sarah would make a nice couple, but the idea didn't sit well with her. Sarah was just too young and immature.

Julien looked even more handsome this morning if that were possible. He wore khaki shorts with sandals, and his arms and legs were brown from the sun. The white t-shirt wasn't exactly snug, but his muscles rippled beneath it and...

"Angelina!" Sarah called, snapping her fingers. "You're all spaced out or something. Julien asked if you're ready to go with us. Of course, if you'd rather not, that's fine too." She ended with a hopeful note.

Angelina came back to earth with a bump. She wasn't prepared to sit idly by slurping coffee while her cousin went off alone with this man. "Sorry. Of course, I'd like to go. Just give me a minute to find my sunglasses and...I wonder Elyse, if you might have a hat I could borrow?" She stood and began to collect their breakfast items and place them on the tray.

"*Bien sûr*." Elyse placed her napkin on the table and rose. "Please, leave the coffee here for me. I think I will enjoy the morning air a little more before I go inside."

Once Angelina was ready, Julien led both women down a well-worn path past the pool and to the front of the chateau where a truck was parked. Angelina had always liked vehicles. She couldn't overhaul an engine or anything, but enjoyed knowing more about them than the average woman.

She saw immediately it was a Renault, an Alaskan, and almost brand new. She wasn't up on all vehicle makes in Europe, but everyone had heard of Renault.

As there were only bucket seats in the front, Sarah hurried forward and hopped into the passenger side, leaving Angelina to clamber into the back. That was fine. She'd rather look at the scenery than make small talk anyway.

It wasn't far to the first field of olive trees, but the terrain was rough. They took the road that was the continuation of the one they'd arrived on. Angelina gripped the armrests to steady herself as they left the pavement and struck out across a rocky track.

After bumping along the road for a time, Julien pulled over and stopped on the verge of a broad field filled with rows of the same feathery trees Angelina had been wondering about. Underneath the heavy, gnarled trunks grass was trimmed and neat, while the silvery canopy spread like an umbrella above.

"They're beautiful." Angelina breathed. She hopped out of the truck before anyone else and walked to the nearest tree. Laying her hand on its bark, she tried to guess how old it was.

"The olive tree is sacred in Provence." Julien slammed his door shut and walked toward her. "Great patience is required to cultivate the olives since they do not bear maximum yield until perhaps thirty years of age."

"So, how old are these ones?" Sarah minced across the rocky ground on her high-heeled sandals, arms outstretched for balance. Julien looked at her feet with narrowed eyes.

He stepped to where she teetered back and forth, and took her arm.

"This grove was planted long before my ancestors took over the estate," he said, leading her to where Angelina stood. "Do you see how wide the perimeter of the trunk is? We can tell much from its size. These trees are several hundred years old."

Sarah clung to him, pulling his arm close to her body. Angelina looked away. It bothered her to watch Sarah fawning over Julien. Instead, she shook herself and walked between the rows of ancient trees, marvelling at their age and beauty.

"I can't go too far," Sarah said in a plaintive voice behind her.

"It might have been wise to wear other shoes, knowing we were going for a tour in a field," Angelina ventured dryly. But there was nothing else to do except get in the truck and see what they could from the vehicle. It would be an easy matter for her to walk here later and stroll through the sighing trees alone.

Without warning, Sarah pitched forward with a shriek, and would have fallen if Julien hadn't caught her.

"*Ouch!*" she yelped as he helped her to stand. Sarah lifted her right foot off the ground and clutched Julien tighter. "I've twisted my ankle or something. It's too painful to stand."

"Don't move," he said, concern causing his voice to grow husky. "I'll carry you." Bending down, Julien lifted her with ease and her arms slid around his neck. She leaned her head on his shoulder, her face tight with pain.

"Oh Sarah, I'm so sorry." Angelina jogged ahead to open the truck door.

Gently, Julien set Sarah on the seat. Then, taking infinite care, he undid her sandal and slipped it from the moaning girl's foot. "It's swelling already I am afraid," he said. Craning his neck, he looked back at Angelina. "We must take her to the house and apply ice."

Stepping back, he closed the door with care and rushed to leap in the other side. It took longer to reach the front door of the chateau than it had when they left, since Julien made an effort to avoid many of the potholes and stones that made the journey rough the first time through.

"Could you open the double doors for us Angelina?" he asked, swivelling around to peer at her in the back. "I'll take Sarah to her room, and we can make her comfortable."

"Yes. Of course."

Angelina took the steps two at a time to be there well before them and stood waiting as Julien reached the landing with the white-faced girl, carrying her as though she wasn't there at all. Despite the pain, Sarah didn't bother to conceal the smug look on her face as she glanced at her cousin. Angelina couldn't help wondering if the ankle was as badly twisted as Sarah was letting on. However, she closed the doors and rushed past the pair as Julien mounted the staircase to the bedrooms. She flung wide Sarah's door and, kicking aside a few articles of clothing strewn about the floor, she plumped up the pillows on the bed for him to lay her cousin down.

This bedroom was more modern than hers, she noticed. Both were pretty and quite Provencal, but this one was not as cozy, she decided. There was a television attached to the wall opposite the bed, the space was larger, and there wasn't a balcony. The room and furnishings were a crisp, clean white, and the headboard was large, square, and quilted. Mirrors hung over the end tables on either side, and another, full-length mirror was propped against the wall beside a large walk-in closet. The obligatory chandelier was present too, but far more modest than the one in the hallway.

Sarah's suitcases were thrown open on the floor and overflowed with brightly patterned clothes. Angelina bent to pick a few of them up.

Julien maneuvered through the door and tenderly laid Sarah on the bed. Angelina grabbed a pillow to cushion and elevate her cousin's foot, and stood looking down at her as Julien left to find ice.

"Oh Angelina," the young woman groaned. "What have I done?" Restlessly, she rolled her head back and forth. "This isn't what I wanted."

"I know." Angelina soothed the girl's brow with her hand. "At least you didn't break your ankle. You'll be back on it after a few days' rest."

"But we only *have* a few days!"

"We have two glorious weeks here, Sarah. And think how Julien will have to hold you in his arms to take you places," Angelina joked, hoping to see a smile tug at Sarah's mouth.

It worked. Her cousin giggled. "It was sweet of him to carry me." She stared at Angelina with wide, blue eyes. "He's really strong. I felt like I was nothing more than a feather. I mean, he practically *jogged* up those stairs," she said, smothering a laugh.

At that moment, the man himself entered the room carrying a towel, two icepacks, a glass, and a bottle of pain medication.

"How's the patient feeling?" he asked, setting the items on the table beside Sarah.

"She's feeling irritated with herself," Sarah answered with a sigh.

Angelina took the ice and wrapped it in the towel to arrange on either side of Sarah's foot, while Julien filled the glass with cold water from the bathroom tap.

"*Voila*," he said. "Take these tablets for the pain and rest a while. You will feel better by this evening. Do you need anything else? A snack perhaps? *Un café au lait?*"

Sarah levered herself up on the pillows to take the pills and grimaced. "Coffee sounds wonderful," she said.

"*Bien*. I shall send Clarisse with some, and a snack as well. My mother went out for a while, but I'm sure she will be up to see you when she returns." He handed Sarah the remote for the TV and moved to the door. "Rest well, *ma chère*."

"Yes, take it easy sweetie. I'll come check on you in a little while." Angelina leaned over to squeeze Sarah's hand as it tapped impatiently on the bed beside her.

"Okay," she said. A small frown appeared between her eyes. "Don't forget about me."

"Never." Angelina smiled and whisked out of the room behind Julien.

Her mind was spinning. With Sarah out of commission for a few days, perhaps she'd have time alone with Julien to discover what he was hiding. What were his true intentions regarding her young cousin? There was no other reason Angelina would want to spend time with the man.

Was there?

CHAPTER 6

Julien was waiting at the top of the stairs. With a glance toward Sarah's door, he motioned for Angelina to come closer.

"Shall we continue the tour, or do you wish to stay at the house?" he asked. He ran fingers through his sandy hair and Angelina was hard-pressed not to imagine herself doing the same. "I didn't want Sarah to feel badly that she could not come with us, but I understand if you wish to rest yourself or remain with her."

"I'd like to see more of your family estate," she said. "I can't do anything more for my cousin at the moment. Can we be back by lunch? I could spend time with her then if that's alright?"

"*Parfait. Bonne idée*," he said, motioning that she walk with him downstairs. "I mean, that is perfect. A good idea. You must forgive me, sometimes I forget to use English when speaking to you and Sarah."

"It's fine. I understood you," she said. "I took French in school, but haven't used it for years...so I've lost a lot now. I enjoy hearing you and your mother speak." They reached the foyer.

"Will you please wait here for me while I relay the message to Clarisse?" Without waiting for her response, he turned and was gone.

Julien certainly appeared to be a caring person, she reflected. Unless it was all an act. She still had grave doubts about him. Promising herself she'd remember to ask Sarah what she knew about his family, she heard the light footsteps of his return and moved to open the door.

"*Bien*, it is done," he said. "I 'ope that she recovers fast. Your cousin was quite excited to come to France." They descended the steps together, but he stepped ahead to open the truck door for her.

"*Merci*." Angelina reached for her seatbelt as he climbed in the other side. "I like your truck. It appears to be a 4-cylinder, twin-turbo diesel with a 6-speed transmission. Is that right? How much horsepower?" She settled back in the cushy seat to watch with satisfaction as his hand dropped away from the key and his mouth fell open with surprise. She looked nonchalantly at the dashboard and noted that the vehicle had every option available to man. *Figures.*

"How could you know that?" Slowly he turned toward her, his face a study in disbelief.

"I have a couple of tricks up my sleeve," she said, brushing imaginary lint off her skirt. "I grew up on a farm where my dad fixed everything that needed fixing. He was a pretty good mechanic and taught me a bit about vehicles."

"Tricks up your—sleeve?" Julien repeated with a frown. "What does this mean?"

She snickered. It wasn't that she was glad Sarah got hurt, but she *was* enjoying this time alone with him. It would serve him right to be put in his place.

"It means, perhaps I know more than you would otherwise think. Even if I am a klutz."

Reaching for his keys again, Julien started the motor, slipped the vehicle into first, and they rolled down the driveway. She admired his strong, capable hand as it rested on the gearshift.

"You are a surprising woman, Angelina." He shook his head and shot her a sideways look. "Very intriguing. Now, would you like to go back to the olives, or should we visit one of the vineyards next?"

Once Angelina stopped blushing at this unexpected praise, she spoke. "I'll walk to the olive grove later today by myself," she said. "But a tour of the vines would be lovely."

"As you wish, *mademoiselle*." He turned in the opposite direction to this morning. "And, in answer to your question, it has 190 horse-power." He patted the dash and grinned at her, his eyes flashing with humour.

"That's great," she said. "Not to mention cup-holders and heated leather seats." She giggled outright then, and he joined her, laughing with a deep resonant tone that made her heart do flips.

"Do you drive?" he asked. He shifted gears as they passed the production buildings and turned onto the main road.

"A little." She had no intention of telling him what

she'd been doing for a living. It would only invite his censure. She'd had enough of that to last her a lifetime.

"What does this mean? A little? Can you drive a standard transmission? Many people who come to Europe from North America cannot, so I must ask."

"I can," she answered.

Nodding, Julien continued. "Good. Then, as long as you have your licence along, you may borrow a vehicle if you wish. Take it in order that you and Sarah may visit the many sights in our area. My mother and I are often engaged elsewhere and cannot accompany you. *D'accord?*"

"*D'accord*," she agreed. "You're sure you can spare it?"

"I will bring it to the house after lunch. It is an older Citroën we keep for running errands. It would please me..." he paused and rubbed the growth on his chin as though to reset his brain, "it would please my *mother* and me, if you would use it."

He lapsed into silence. They drove along the pavement for only a mile or so before he signalled to the right and pulled onto another worn track in the sandy-coloured soil. They drove steadily higher toward the rocky limestone ridge. The chateau, and buildings that comprised the Belliveau Estate, could be seen glimmering below them in the morning sunlight. The vehicle bumped along for some distance, until the sight of the busy road behind them faded into the distance. The vineyard stretched all around them, so close Angelina could have leaned from the window and filled her hands with tantalizing grapes, if she'd wanted. Julien pulled the truck over and shut it off. But he didn't reach for the door handle.

He paused a long moment, his hands on the wheel and his head bowed. Angelina could sense the rigidity of his body as he wrestled with what he wanted to say. Was it about Sarah? His mother? Maybe the problems she'd heard him discussing the night before?

"I..." he stopped and then started again, "I want to..." he looked up and stared at her. "...ask if you would like to see the vines up close?" The final question came out in a rush. Angelina knew very well that wasn't what he'd wanted to say, but whatever it had been, he'd changed his mind.

"I would," she answered, staring at him in return. He fidgeted with the dials on the truck's radio, even though it wasn't on.

Still, they sat. A crazy thought crossed her mind. Was he going to reach out and take her hand? But with a flourish, he swung around, opened the driver's door, and came striding around the truck to help her out. She didn't need help, but she accepted his arm and slid to the ground beside him.

For a moment, he was so close that they almost touched. She took a deep, involuntary breath, blinked, and shuffled to the side. Julien became brisk and very much the knowledgeable tour guide.

"If you step this way *mademoiselle*, you will see a fine example of the vine, *Mourvedre*. When expertly combined with other varieties of grapes, grown here on the estate, they create one of the best *vin rosé* in Provence." He waved his arms to illustrate his words as he strode between vines that hung heavy with dark, purple fruit.

Leaves rustled in a slight breeze that swung down

from the rocky ledge above. She followed Julien, marvelling at the scent of the ripe grapes.

Angelina stumbled over a rock before she posed her questions. "How do the vines grow in such rough terrain? I grew up on a farm and, forgive me for saying so, but this soil looks terrible."

Julien chuckled. "This is true, the earth does not look productive, but in fact, the vines do best in ground that makes them struggle. They need drainage that is not possible in soils that 'old the water." Dropping down to kneel he grabbed a clump and examined them, leaning in and bringing them to his nose. He closed his eyes and took a deep breath.

"Wine has been made in Provence for 2600 years. The flavour of these grapes is concentrated and flavourful." He stood, dusting off the knee where he'd knelt. "The vines require sunshine, not too much rain, warm days, and cool evenings. The Mediterranean climate provides all this. Shall we continue to walk back up the path?" Angelina nodded and led the way to the vehicle.

"So, where do you come from?" Julien asked as they walked along the trail. "Sarah told us a little about your sister, I believe, but we know nothing about you."

Angelina kicked at a clump of grass with her sneaker, "I come from one of the prairie provinces of Canada. Saskatchewan to be exact. I grew up on a farm where my parents did a little of everything to earn a living. We raised cattle and grain, had a big garden, and kept a few chickens. Not too exciting."

"*Au contraire*," he said. "It sounds so unlike how I grew up that it becomes quite fascinating." He picked up a branch that lay across the path and swung it at his side. "And, your parents, are they still alive?"

"Why, yes," Angelina answered with a little surprise. Mom and Dad were only in their fifties, after all. "They sold the farm and retired early, due to Dad's heart. But they're both great. You?" She caught herself and babbled on. "I mean, of course your *mother* is alive. We just had breakfast together." She giggled.

"*Oui, ma mère est bonne.*" Julien whipped the stick at the long grass swaying in the breeze beside him and it was a long while before he went on. "My father died on March twentieth." He slashed at the grass until it was broken and dangling. "That was roughly four months ago."

Angelina stopped and clasped her hands. "Oh Julien! I'm so sorry. I had no idea. Sarah didn't tell me."

He shrugged. "Of course, 'ow could you know such a thing. Thank you for your concern, but I am fine. It is my mother I worry about." As he turned away and continued walking Angelina considered the way his voice had changed. He didn't appear to be 'fine' at all.

"And do you have other siblings? Besides the sister who could not come?" He glanced at her. She saw the pain of loss in his eyes, plus something else. He was tense again, but it was obvious he didn't want to discuss such matters with her. They barely knew one another.

"There's just Marcie and me," she said, trudging down the other half of the vehicle track. "We've always been close. She and her husband found out they were pregnant the day before she was about to come here."

"*Oui*, that is what Sarah told us. You will be an aunt," he looked at her, his face lighting up in a grin. "I am glad for her and for you. You can teach this child about the inner workings of trucks."

Angelina laughed. He was teasing her again and she found that she liked it. "I will," she agreed. "Do you have a brother or sister?" They fell into an easy stride. Although the sun was growing hot on her back, Elyse's hat kept her from becoming overwhelmed.

"One of each. My sister, Lia, lives in Marseille with her husband, Mathéo, and son, Mylan." He caught her eye again. "She teaches at *une école primaire*, a school for young children, and apparently likes names that begin with the letter M." They exchanged smiles. He really was quite humorous.

Julien sobered. "And I 'ave a younger brother, Raphaël who works with me 'ere. He 'as friends in Italy and left to visit them the day we returned. He will not be back for one or two days yet. You and Sarah will meet 'im soon."

"How nice for Elyse that you all live so close to her. It's something my parents often mention, although Marcie is in a city two hours' drive away."

They reached the end of the road where it turned both right and left. Angelina peered up into the chalky ridges and scattered boulders that formed the eastern skyline. A huge bird soared high above.

"Look." She caught his eye and pointed. "What is it?"

"It is Bonelli's eagle," he said, following her gaze.

"The bird belongs to someone?" she asked, incredulously. Angelina whirled around to face him, and her straw hat went flying in a sudden gust of wind. Stooping, Julien caught it before it rolled away and brought it to her, standing close enough to place the hat back on her head.

She held her breath. He was so close, the scent of his cologne drifted over her. It was spicy and intoxicating. Julien lingered a minute, fussing with her hair. He pushed it behind her ears, away from her face so that the wind couldn't steal *le chapeau* from her again. But why was he taking so long? Her eyes flickered up to him, but he avoided her gaze.

"No one owns the bird," he said abruptly, moving away. "It is just the name of the species. I don't know why. Shall we go back? There is time to show you a little of the winery before a late lunch, if you like?"

"Sure."

They said nothing more as they trudged back to the truck. Angelina wondered if Julien had felt the same electricity she had. Probably not, with his focus on Sarah. Angelina had to keep in mind that she had a bigger purpose in being here.

Holding the hat on her head against the breeze, she waved away his help, and clambered into the truck herself. She didn't need his help or a man in her life to mess things up.

CHAPTER 7

The remainder of the morning was interesting, but uneventful. Julien parked outside the shop where the family's wines and olive oils were for sale. After they had gone inside, Angelina was introduced to a young woman, Anna, who according to Julien, was the guide for all the estate's tours since she spoke several languages fluently.

"I will leave you in Anna's capable hands. *À plus tard, Mademoiselle*," he said with all the warmth of a drill sergeant.

Angelina half expected Julien to bow and click his heels like she'd imagined him doing back at the airport in Montreal. It was as though they'd just met all over again. He was retreating from any attempt at the friendship they'd formed. She squinted at his back as he hustled through a door and disappeared. *See you later, indeed monsieur*.

Angelina wandered around the shop, waiting while Anna finished with the first group of the day. Other people including a couple from Australia, and a family of five from somewhere in the USA, milled around the store with her. Clearly, they were all about to be led on a tour of the buildings together.

It was fine. She hadn't expected Julien to take the whole day off just to show her around, but she couldn't help pondering if this would have happened had Sarah been here. Angelina looked at her watch. At this rate, she wouldn't get back to the chateau until well after lunch. She hadn't realised she'd be taking an organized tour and wondered how long it lasted. Maybe she could duck out partway through.

However, spending the next couple of hours with Anna, and the tour, was enjoyable, if a little anti-climactic. As they wove their way through people in white coats and hats, busy at work, Anna explained how the grapes were harvested, selected, fermented, aged, and bottled. It was all very interesting, but Angelina found her mind wandering. When eventually they stood at a long bar, chiselled from what looked to be an enormous oak beam, and waiting to begin the sampling portion of the tour, she begged off.

A young man directed her to the exit, and she stepped into the bright sunlight of a Provencal afternoon. She'd dangled the hat from her hand while indoors, but now she jammed it on her head and began the long uphill march to the chateau.

She was dusty and hot by the time she turned the corner and caught sight of the impressive home with the sparkling pool beyond. The water looked so inviting. A dip would feel pretty good right about now—if she could swim.

A car was parked out front. Perhaps this was the one Julien had meant for her to drive? She took a turn around the vehicle. It was a tiny, yellow Citroën. How appropriate. But now, it was time to check on Sarah. With gratitude, she escaped the heat as she ducked inside the cool corridor of the chateau.

Mounting the staircase two steps at a time, Angelina padded silently across the plush carpeting and dropped her borrowed hat and sunglasses off in her room before knocking at Sarah's door. She could hear the TV blaring.

"Come in," Sarah called over the noise.

"Hi." Angelina spied a chair and dragged it over to sit beside her cousin. "How are you feeling now?"

Sarah pushed herself higher up on the pillows and rolled her eyes. "It sucks. But the ankle doesn't throb anymore, so I guess that's a good sign." She looked away to examine a few magazines someone had thoughtfully provided and shuffled them back and forth across the bed. "So, what did you do today? Were you with Julien?" She reached for the remote and muted the show she'd been watching.

Of course, that would be Sarah's first question.

"He showed me the vineyard and then dropped me off to take a tour with a bunch of other visitors without a backward glance. Does that make you happy?" Angelina purposely tried to downplay the excursion to see the vines and emphasize the public tour. As she'd hoped, Sarah brightened.

"Was it good? Did you learn a lot? Did you drink some wine?"

"Hang on." Laughing, Angelina raised a hand of protest. "It was interesting although I was thinking too much about you to really have much information sink in. I came back here before they tasted the wine."

"Oh, too bad, but I guess you're not supposed to swallow anyway." Sarah's head drooped and she fiddled with the magazines again. "So, you were alone with him until then though. Do you think he was worried about me?"

"Yes. Of course, he was worried." Angelina edged her chair closer and lowered her voice. "Why don't you tell me what you know of this family? We haven't had a chance to talk or be alone since we met at the airport. I know nothing about the people I'm staying with."

Sarah's brows rose in realization. "I guess you don't, do you?" She held a hand over her mouth to stifle a yawn, and sliding down onto her pillows, she began. "The Belliveau's were in Quebec to visit Elyse's sister. I think Julien was trying to get his mom away from the house for a while, because her husband just died. Oh...I probably didn't tell you that either, did I?"

Angelina shook her head.

"Sorry. Well, it's only been a few months since the man's funeral and Elyse has been having a hard time coming to terms with it. Julien's a great guy though." She started to warm to the subject and colour stole into her cheeks. "He really cares about his mom. It's sweet, don't you think?"

Again, Angelina answered with a nod.

"Anyway, my aunt and uncle were invited over to where they were staying for a garden party and *voila*, we met. The families spent a lot of time together after that and I got to know Julien super well. I love his accent." She closed her eyes and then fluttered them open. "But there's something weird about him too. Some big, dark secret that he won't talk about."

Sarah stared at Angelina with large innocent eyes. "I overheard them arguing about it once."

"Oh?" Angelina couldn't help but be interested.

"Yeah. I was hoping Julien would go swimming with me, so I went looking for him. They were in his bedroom with the door shut, but their voices were so loud I could hear them. Elyse told him she wanted to know the truth, and Julien said there was nothing more to say on the subject. But obviously there was. They kept talking for quite a while."

"You didn't listen at the door though, right?" Angelina was concerned her niece had intentionally eavesdropped.

"Of course not! What do you think I am? A snoop?" In spite of her indignation, Sarah giggled. "I left right away, so that's all I heard. But it sounds strange, don't you think?"

"Whatever it is, they'll work it out." Angelina smiled. "Now, how about some lunch. I'm starving. Shall I go down and bring up something to share?"

As she left the room on her errand, Angelina wondered about what Sarah had said. It certainly seemed to tie in with Julien's phone conversation the night before. It was obvious he was keeping the whole truth from his mother—whatever it was.

In looking for the kitchen, she walked into the dining room, knowing she could access it from there. She hadn't been anywhere else in this grand home and didn't want to burst into the wrong room by accident. Elyse stood at the far end, staring out a window at the vast expanse of garden beyond. She turned as Angelina entered and came toward her with arms outstretched.

The lady appeared to have been crying. She held a tissue in one hand, and then, seeming to realise it was there, she stuffed it into a pocket of her long, flowing dress.

"*Bonjour*," she said, a faint smile crossing her lips. "I 'ope you 'ad a nice tour of the estate? And 'ow is Sarah?" She grasped Angelina's hands.

"*Bonjour*. It was an interesting morning, thank you. And Sarah's not in any pain at present. I was just going to see about some lunch for the two of us."

"Of course. When I tapped at 'er door she was sleeping, so I did not disturb her." Elyse led the way into the largest, longest kitchen Angelina had ever seen. It was modern and bright, almost clinical. The same older man that had brought them the salad was there, washing vegetables at an extensive sink. He dried his hands with a towel and turned to them expectantly.

"This is Armand, our wonderful chef, but 'e is not kept busy enough with so few of us 'ere now." Elyse took a deep breath before continuing. "Armand, this is our guest from Canada, Angelina. I should 'ave introduced you last night. My apologies, I was not thinking."

"*Enchanté*." The man nodded and Angelina returning the greeting, extended her hand to shake. She loved how Elyse pronounce the man's name.

"Armand, do you 'ave something that Angelina and her cousin, Sarah, could eat for lunch?"

"Certainly, madam. It will take only a few moments to prepare."

"*Merci*."

Elyse gestured to a small table and chairs close to where they had entered the kitchen. They sat down to wait. Angelina marvelled at the facilities. There was an island that ran the full length of the room, and on either side of it were gleaming, silver and black appliances, at least two of each sort. These were flush with a wall of white cupboards that would undoubtedly house a wealth of dishes and equipment.

On the other side were a series of sinks and a massive gas range, all set into a black marble countertop. Wide latticed windows were set deeply into the wall and at intervals along the northeast side. She could see the mountainous terrain arching into the sky outside.

But the most amazing focus of the room was at the far end where a short staircase led up to meet stone steps that were mounted against the wall.. Each step was a separate rock affixed, somehow, to the wall leading to where they disappeared above.

"It is called a rolling stone staircase," Elyse said, following Angelina's gaze. "We had the chateau updated four years ago. It is unusual, *n'est-ce pas?*"

"*Oui*," said Angelina. "It's amazing." Her thoughts wandered to the wealth these people must have to afford such extravagance. Yet, they both appeared nonplussed about it. They were as down-to-earth as her own folks back home, as far as she could tell.

"I would like to tell you two things and ask that you pass them along to Sarah. The first, is that *un voisin*, a neighbour and fellow vitiner, will be 'ere for dinner tonight, with 'is family. Second, and most important, is that Julien and I 'ave decided to give a small dinner party here, two evenings from now." Elyse twisted her hands in her lap. "My son, Raphaël, will arrive 'ome that day, and I would like to give you and Sarah a party, to welcome you both to France."

She gave Angelina a wan smile. "We 'ave not had much laughter around 'ere lately. It is time to live again." Elyse gave her usual, expressive shrug.

Impulsively, Angelina stood and wrapped the older woman in an embrace. She felt Elyse's thin shoulders heave as the woman took a deep breath.

"*Merci beaucoup*, Elyse. A party would be fun. It's so sweet of you to do that for us." She sat back down.

"Armand will do the work." Elyse retrieved the tissue and dabbed at her eyes. "All we 'ave to do is look pretty and enjoy ourselves." She stood up and called to the chef. "*C'est vrai*, Armand?"

Armand, who was clattering about the kitchen, flipped something in a pan on the stovetop, and gave Elyse a little salute. "It is true," he agreed with a grin, then looked pointedly at Angelina. "Your food is ready, *mademoiselle*."

Angelina jumped up to thank him and stood looking at the tray in awe. He had prepared a fabulous lunch in a short amount of time. There were two glasses of cold orange juice, golden omelettes lightly sprinkled with chopped chives, tiny green salads in bowls on the side and two thin slivers of what looked like chocolate cheesecake.

"It's too pretty to eat!" she exclaimed, earning a chuckle from Armand. "Are those actually flowers in the salad?" She leaned closer. There were tiny, velvety mauve and fuchsia blossoms nestled in the greens.

"*Oui,*" he said. Clearly, he was pleased at her attention to his presentation. "They are *fleurs de pensée*. I believe you call them, pansies, in English."

"It looks delicious. *Merci* Armand." She beamed at him as she hoisted the tray. "And thank you for the chat, Elyse. Did you wish to join us?"

"*Non, merci,*" the lady said. The silky material of her dress swirled around her ankles as she walked with Angelina back through the formal dining room. "I 'ave many things to do to prepare for tonight and for the party. It is something to look forward to, yes?"

"It certainly is," Angelina said.

"Dinner will be at seven," said Elyse. With a wave, the woman left her in the hallway and Angelina carefully plodded up the stairs with the tray, watching lest she spill the juice. She pushed open the door to her cousin's room and, in the gloom, saw the girl struggling to stand up.

"I'm tired of this confinement already," Sarah said, hopping unsteadily to the bathroom and shutting the door.

Angelina set the food on the night table and went to open one of Sarah's curtains a crack, so they could at least see what they were eating. She looked out at the sparkling pool from this north-facing window and was grateful for her balcony.

"You'll be healed in no time," she assured Sarah, as the girl crawled onto the bed again. "And, I have news for you." She picked up the tray and examined it closer, realizing it had folding legs to fit over one's lap as they sat. *Perfect.*

Sarah pulled herself upright and lifted her hands out

of the way as Angelina placed the lunch over her legs and rearranged the contents. She removed the food meant for herself and sat down on the chair next to the bed.

"News? And this lunch looks awesome." Sarah grabbed her fork and cut into the omelette. "Mmm, it's delicious." Cheese and mushrooms oozed onto her plate.

Angelina's mouth watered. She reached for her own plate and set it on her knee. "Some friends and neighbours are coming for supper tonight and—Elyse and Julien are throwing us a party in two days' time."

Sarah's head snapped up with delight. "Ooh, a party! Where? Here? Who's coming? What will I wear?" Her eyes flicked to the bulging suitcases on the floor. "Maybe we should go shopping?"

"Whoa, hang on," Angelina laughed. "Yes, here. Two days from now. I have no idea who will attend. And, you have a wealth of cocktail dresses with you just begging to be worn. I'm sure you'll have no trouble finding something suitable."

She paused to take another bite. "Did you know Julien has a sister and brother?"

"Yes, of course. I've even seen pictures of them," Sarah said between mouthfuls. "I don't think the brother is as hot as Julien, but maybe he'll look better in real life. I guess we'll find out, won't we?" She looked Angelina with mischief in her eyes. "Maybe you could have him."

"You can't just hand a man around like a second helping of potatoes, Sarah. They *do* have a say in the matter." She was amused with the girl. "Besides, I don't *want* him. I've no interest in men at the moment, but a party would be fun. Perhaps Julien's sister will come." Scraping up the last of her omelette, she had a sudden urge to lick the plate. She set the dish down hurriedly and picked up her salad. Chef Armand had made a dressing that was light and flavourful; even the flowers were tasty.

Sarah chattered on about what she might wear and how cute Julien would look. Angelina only half listened. Her input wasn't required. Sarah was a one-girl show.

By the time they'd finished eating, Angelina was looking to escape the incessant detailing of her cousin's wardrobe, what Sarah's friends always said about her many outfits and beauty, and how everyone back home was going to be jealous. Angelina loaded her dishes back onto the tray, gathered up Sarah's, and told her she was heading out for a walk.

"But it'll be boiling hot outside," Sarah protested. "You wouldn't think so in here, because of the air-conditioning they must have, but it's really hot in the south of France. Don't you know that?"

"I know it. See you later, Cuz." She fixed a smile on her face and picked up the tray. "I'm sure Julien will carry you downstairs for dinner later."

Sarah reached for the remote as Angelina pushed the door open with her bottom and fled into the hall. She planned to return the dishes to the kitchen, wash them if allowed, and go for a walk, despite the heat. A ruby-red, two-piece bathing suit lurked at the bottom of her armoire. She planned to use it, even if only to paddle in the shallow end—if there *was* a shallow end of the large rectangular pool.

Armand and another woman were busy in the kitchen and shooed her away from washing the dishes. Thanking the chef again for the wonderful meal, she wandered back through the dining room and upstairs. It would be smart, she thought, to put her two-piece bathing suit on under her dress and grab a towel, so she wouldn't have to come up here again.

Sunlight streamed into the beautiful bedroom. She'd kept the heavy drapes on one side of the room closed against the heat of the day, but couldn't bring herself to entirely shut out the view toward the west. She crossed to the window facing the front of the chateau to grab her book from the bedside table where she'd left it. If it was too hot to walk, at least she could sit by the pool and read.

Moments later, Angelina was dressed. She intended to walk back to the olive grove and take her time among the trees. Grabbing the hat and sunglasses off the bed, she made her way outside. It really was like walking into an oven—that first breath of hot air, almost shocking.

For interest's sake, she chose a path through the flower garden to the south of the chateau. It led in the direction of the olive groves, and she crunched through light gravel that was flanked on either side by a low box hedge.

Dusky, red roses climbed an overhead trellis at the corner of the chateau and the entrance of the garden. Angelina stooped to breathe deeply of their spicy scent. A lazy bee wobbled past, making his way from one flower to the next. The heat was fine for him, but Sarah was right, it was too hot for a hike to the olives today. Instead, Angelina meandered along the winding path, trying to name a few of the many varieties of plants that grew in ordered profusion here.

There were huge clumps of a green shrub that looked familiar. With a delicate tug she grasped a tall frond and pulled. The aroma of rosemary filled her senses. That's what it was! She hadn't known they could grow so large. Ahead, expansive flower beds edged with tiny, low-lying plants, and bursting with multi-coloured blooms, stretched up to the house and back to a long rock wall. She recognized hibiscus, gardenias, and daylilies, their colours creating a patchwork of beauty in this oasis. To the east, beyond the wall, lay the range of craggy limestone peaks.

A trickle of perspiration made its way down her spine, and she thought of the pool. Backtracking, she made her way to the familiar terrace and collapsed into a chair in the shade. Laying her book on the table, she enjoyed the sunlight shimmering off the mirrored waters for a moment. She scanned the area. There was no one around; no one to snicker at her inability to swim. It would only take five minutes to hop into the pool, cool herself, and then dry off before settling into a lounger with the book.

Angelina kicked off her shoes, tossed her hat and sunglasses onto the chair, and peeled her dress over her head as she stood. Exchanging her cover up garment for a towel, she dropped it beside her before she lowered herself to the edge of the pool and dangled her legs in the refreshing waters. Easing her entire body into the water, she twisted around to hold the lip of the cement with her fingers and allowed her body to float in the warm blue depths. How relaxing.

Her toes stretched for the bottom as she pushed herself away from the hard wall and into the gentle rocking motion of the ripples. She lifted her chin and enjoyed the feeling of weightlessness. It was disconcerting that she couldn't touch the bottom though, so she extended her arms to reach for the cement perimeter.

Without warning, a silhouette rose over her, and the sun was blocked. Before she could focus on the shape, or grasp for the edge of the pool again, the shadow hurtled over her head and plunged into the water with a resounding splash. Waves surged over her face and entered her nose. She took a strangled breath and inhaled water. Spluttering, her fingers lost their tentative grasp on the wall. Flailing her arms and legs, she fought to lift her face above the undulating swell as panic gripped her heart.

Then, hands slid beneath her arms, and she was propelled up and into the air. She took a ragged breath. Relief washed over her as she realised someone had come to her rescue. The fact that it was the same someone that had nearly caused her to drown, only hit her later. For now, she was grateful and, although her eyes were blurry and no doubt streaming mascara, her fingers grasped eagerly for the solid foundation of the pool.

"I apologise," Julien's voice floated into her watery ears. "It is plain to me now, you cannot swim. I am so sorry I startled you and caused you to lose your grip."

Yeah, that was accurate. She was definitely losing her grip around this place. She leaned her forehead against the rough confines of the pool wall and coughed. Slowly, she turned to face him, keeping one hand firmly fixed on the wall at her back.

"You scared the life out of me!" she accused. "Do you always have to do a crazy cannonball dive into the pool?"

"*Always?*" he repeated. His mouth curved upward, and it appeared as though it was taking effort to school it into a grim line. "You 'ave been observing me from afar?" He was mocking her again. She could have drowned, and he was snickering.

"I don't think it's very funny to drown your guests." Tossing her head, she sent droplets of water flying in all directions. She ignored his question as to whether she had been spying on him, swung around and began to edge along the side. Her eyes locked on a nearby set of steps and a railing that she could use to pull herself out with dignified grace, instead of attempting to lunge from the pool directly in front of him.

"No, *mademoiselle*, you are correct." His laughing voice followed her. "It is not funny. I might 'ave trouble sleeping tonight if I allowed my lovely guest to perish."

Angelina responded with a loud *humph* of disgust, but her efforts to pull herself to the railing were thwarted by Julien himself. He took her arms, disentangled them from the edge, and rotated her around to face him. She found herself staring at a broad expanse of chest, lightly dusted with hairs before she watched his handsome face descending to hers. Her mind warned her to escape—to duck away, submerge herself, to do anything to evade this advance. Except her heart leaped in her chest as she watched as his lips grow closer.

As though in slow motion, she felt his mouth sweep

across her own. It was light. Nothing more than a tantalising brush of his lips over hers. Despite her body being underwater, Angelina felt heat stir deep in her stomach. Her eyes widened, meeting his as he pulled back and, after ensuring her one hand gripped the edge, abruptly released her again. The expression in his eyes looked as surprised as her own must be.

"*Je suis desole*," he said, his voice sounding distant and confused. "I mean—I am sorry, Angelina. For frightening you and..." he paused. "Well, for..." Treading water, he moved away, yet his eyes remained locked upon her own.

Angelina raised dripping fingers to her lips. She had a sudden, crazy urge to push herself across the few inches that separated them and press her mouth back against his.

She shook her head, as though to clear the lethargy that slowed her thinking and addled her brain.

"It's okay," she mumbled. Her words sounded sticky, as though she'd dragged them into the air, where enunciating every syllable was an effort. Silence hung between them.

With a deep breath she mastered herself and spoke louder than she'd intended. "But I'm not thanking you for saving my life when you're the one who almost caused me to lose it."

He grinned, and the spell was broken.

"Naturally," he said. "Will you be alright now? If so, I shall continue my swim and will meet you on dry land in a few minutes."

"Of course. I don't care what you do." Listening to him chuckle behind her, she wondered who she was trying to convince with her bold proclamation. Angelina grabbed the rail, pulled herself from the water and hurried to pick up her towel. As she did so, a flicker of movement caught her eye. She glanced up and could have sworn she saw the curtains in Sarah's room slide shut.

Inwardly, she groaned. Had her cousin seen what had taken place over the last few minutes? Surely not. If Sarah was angry and demanded an account of all that had taken place, it would be the final blow to Angelina's pride.

What would possess Sarah to get out of bed and lurk behind a curtain at the window? Surely the girl wasn't feeling *that* possessive of Julien—and suspicious of her? Yet, Angelina had already seen evidence to suggest that Sarah was insecure and jealous. If Sarah had seen Julien and her kissing...no, she couldn't have. That situation would be impossible to clarify. She couldn't even explain it to herself, let alone Sarah.

Crossing the hot tiles with her towel, she rubbed herself down with unnecessary violence and flopped into a chair. She felt flushed and hot, not at all how she should be feeling after taking a dip in the pool to cool down. Picking up the hat, she fanned herself before yanking it onto her head, sliding on her sunglasses, and picking up the novel. She settled back in the chair, put her feet on a bench across from her, forced herself to open the book, and removed the bookmark.

It was hard to concentrate. After reading the same passage over five times, she gave up. The sounds of splashing were distracting and, finally, with a finger holding her page, she let the book drop to her lap as she scanned the surface of the pool. Julien's dark head bobbed against the blueness of the water as, one after the other, he did his laps.

She slumped and tipped the brim of the hat low over her eyes to shield him from view. Julien was interested in Sarah, not her, she told herself. She had no interest in falling for someone as unscrupulous as him. The fact that he had been brazen enough to kiss her showed how unprincipled he was.

After all, he'd brought Sarah all this way, just to become his plaything. Those were the actions of a player, a womanizer. Granted, she hadn't seen that side of him yet, but she was sure she would. The mere fact that he could kiss her, while stringing Sarah along, was proof.

So deep was she in thought, that she failed to notice Julien clamber from the pool until he stood before her, a puddle of water forming around his feet.

"You 'ave forgiven me, I 'ope?"

With a jolt of shock, she sat bolt upright and made a vain attempt to catch her book before it hit the tiles. She bent to retrieve her novel.

Drawing a cleansing breath, she avoided his eyes and answered with what she hoped was a prim, disinterested answer. "I forgive you, so please don't feel you need to hang around. I'm perfectly fine." She opened the book to a page, any page, and pretended to read with great enthusiasm.

"I probably needed a dose of chlorine anyway," she continued. "It's likely done me a world of good." She maintained her study of the pages that swam in front of her, willing him to leave.

A great guffaw of laughter caused her to jump again. Julien scraped a chair over the tiles and threw himself into it, still scrubbing a towel up and down his muscular legs.

"You are like no one else I 'ave ever met, *mademoiselle* Angelina. I am glad to 'ear you have suffered no ill effects and were refreshed by your sudden dip. Still, I was in the wrong, and…I am sorry." He rose to his feet and walked away. "I shall check on your cousin. Please, enjoy your time out 'ere. I will see you at dinner."

Angelina stole a look at his retreating back. He'd slung the wet towel over one broad shoulder and was sliding into a pair of flipflops before entering the chateau. The second he was gone; a strange sense of loss overcame her.

That was ridiculous. She tossed her head and lowered her eyes to her book, but it was no use trying to read. Her mind kept going over two questions that competed against one another in her mind.

What exactly was he sorry about? The near drowning, or the kiss?

CHAPTER 8

Angelina saw no one on the lower level as she tiptoed up to the sanctuary of her room half an hour later, but could hear the murmur of voices from her cousin's partially open door as she came along the hallway. She halted in midstride. Julien was in there. He was probably reassuring Sarah that he had eyes only for her. The thought left a bitter taste in Angelina's mouth, and she snorted involuntarily.

Whoops! Had they heard her? She shot a frantic glance into the room. What she saw caused her heart to contract.

Julien stood among the suitcases at the foot of the bed and Sarah leaned into his arms, her hands entwined in his hair, face upturned for a kiss. They hadn't heard her. Angelina fumbled with the handle to her private space, dashed inside, and leaned against the door breathing heavily.

Why hadn't she broken up the tableau next door? That was her whole reason for coming here, wasn't it?

She wanted to calmly prevent that sort of intimacy. Instead, she felt like a jealous schoolgirl with her heart and body paralyzed by pain. Was she developing feelings for the man? Absolutely not, that could not be allowed to happen. She had to get a grip on herself.

Unsteadily, she stepped toward the balcony as she heard Sarah's door close, and footsteps retreat down the corridor. She needed fresh air. Dropping onto the one small chair by the railing, she pushed hair away from her flushed cheeks and tried to relax. The heat had not released its grip on the afternoon and the ground continued to bake. She lifted her face to the relentless sun and allowed it to wash over her.

What was happening? Why did she care who Julien kissed? She'd assumed he was a player before she even left Canada, and nothing had happened to change that opinion. Angelina struggled to push down all thoughts of Julien's small kindnesses.

So, maybe he was a sweet guy and good to his mother, it still didn't alter the fact that he had barely finished grabbing her in the pool before he hurried upstairs to kiss Sarah.

This was about her cousin, not Julien. Angelina resolved, from now on, to be a better bodyguard. She allowed herself a brief lightening of spirit at this pronouncement and got to her feet.

Moving inside, she shut the door against the warmth, and went to stand before her closet feeling determined to prepare for dinner with extra attention to her appearance. Company was coming and she needed confidence to face Julien after what had happened today.

She'd overcome far greater obstacles than this. This was nothing compared to proving herself behind the wheel of a truck with twenty men watching for her to fail. She could easily handle this before breakfast, so to speak.

Twenty-five minutes later, she examined her appearance in the full-length mirror she'd found hiding behind the fluffy white bathrobe that hung on the bathroom door. Her hair cascaded down her back in glossy, black waves, and her makeup was impeccable. The shimmery mauve shadow she'd chosen, enhanced the emerald flecks in her eyes and a little mascara had lengthened her already long, thick lashes. A touch of blush and some lipstick perfectly matched an outfit she'd purchased on a whim not long before Bryan had disappeared.

It was a pretty little dress. She twirled to admire the effect of the full, knee-length skirt, fitted waist, and short, poufy, diaphanous sleeves. A little more revealing than she might have liked, but the overall effect of the deep fuchsia chiffon against her pale skin and dark hair was striking. Even if she did say so herself. She only had the same, flat sandals to wear, but if she made a point not to look at herself below the knee, she could pretend they were glittering stilettoes instead.

Descending the staircase, she heard loud jovial voices emanating from a room to her right that she'd not been in before. She stepped inside and quietly took stock, before being noticed.

An older, grey-haired man stood with Julien at the far end of the beautifully decorated living room. Contemporary, leather furniture surrounded the focal point of the space—a huge creamy brick fireplace. Heavy beams ran from one end of the room to the other and full-length windows cast rays of sunlight into the area without needing the ornate lamps set on the many end tables.

Sarah had a chair all to herself. Her foot was propped up on an ottoman that had been moved into a handy position. Elyse sat in another soft-looking chair, sipping a narrow glass of pinkish liquid, and two other women rested comfortably on the sofa across from her, each holding a similar fluted glass. One of them looked up as Angelina walked forward. Her face was lined, but beautiful. Her eyes brightened as she jumped to her feet and tapped the shoulder of the younger woman seated beside her.

"Bonjour, Mademoiselle Fisk," she said, not waiting for a formal introduction, but claiming Angelina's hand in her own with genuine friendliness. "I am Madeleine Malbec, and this is my daughter Natalie. We own the vineyard several kilometres further west of the Belliveaus. I am so pleased to meet you. Sarah has been telling us of all the times you took care of her as she grew up."

Angelina felt the warmth of the lady's greeting and collected a drink from a group of glasses that sat on a silver platter near Elyse. "*Enchantée Madame Malbec,*" she said with her best French accent. "I'm happy to meet you as well."

Beaming, the lady beckoned to her companion who uncrossed long, bare legs, but made no move to rise. She lifted a languid arm to greet Angelina with a distinct lack of enthusiasm.

"*Je suis Natalie Malbec. Enchantée.*" The young woman didn't bother to translate her greeting into English and appeared quite bored with the entire proceeding. Her voice, issuing from unusually plump, glossy lips, was flat and monotone. She accepted Angelina's outstretched hand with ill grace, a slight frown furrowing her brow as they made contact.

Angelina held the woman's limp fingers for only a second, but it was enough to sense the chill that emanated from her. For some reason, Natalie was *not* pleased that she and Sarah were guests of the Belliveau's. She wondered why. Then, following the woman's gaze as she relaxed back into the furniture, Angelina understood.

Beneath a thick fringe of platinum hair, Natalie's blue eyes rested upon Julien in the manner of a coyote sizing up a mouse. He would make a nice light snack and was most definitely her prey. Considering that, it was understandable that two attractive young women living under his roof for days on end was not an appealing state of affairs.

Angelina glanced at Sarah and saw that her cousin had come to the same conclusion. They caught one another's eyes and for a fraction of a second, Sarah's eyebrows lifted, and her head jerked toward Julien before she spoke.

"Madame Malbec just told me that there are many family-run olive groves in the area, like theirs, and that most of them bring their olives here, to the Belliveau mills, to be pressed." Sarah leaned forward and used two hands to move her ankle into a more comfortable position. Someone had thoughtfully placed an extra cushion close for her to use. Angelina could easily guess who.

"Oh, that's interesting. It's a whole other world here." Angelina perched on a loveseat near Sarah as the two older women continued to chat knowledgeably about the business of olive groves and vineyards. It was plain they led active roles in their families' industry.

While Elyse described the troubles of the previous April, where unusual frosts had affected the flowering of the olive trees, Angelina's gaze wandered to Julien. Apart from a nod of acknowledgement when she'd entered the room, he hadn't paid the women any notice whatsoever.

He leaned against the fireplace; a glass of *vin rosé* held precariously in one hand as he gestured with his other to illustrate the story he was telling. He wore tan-coloured jacket and trousers with a crisp, white, button-up shirt, undone at the neck. His hair was combed straight back, but then fell over one eye giving him a rakish look that was most appealing.

Angelina sighed. Unconsciously, her fingertips touched her lips, imagining the light kiss they'd shared this afternoon. Without warning, Julien glanced across the room as though sensing her regard. Their eyes met and held, and Angelina's heart beat a rapid tattoo in her chest.

She caught herself with a toss of her head. This man might be the picture of good looks, self-assurance, and urbanity, but she would not be moved by mere attraction. Men had been nothing but trouble for her lately and she looked away.

"And what do you do in Canada?" Madame Malbec was asking.

Angelina came back to earth with a thump, realizing the question had been directed at her. What *did* she do? She wasn't keen on telling them, to be frank. Even back home, when people learned of her profession, they didn't handle it well. They expected someone or something different when they thought of a truck driver. Not a person like her.

"Actually, I..." But she was saved from having to answer by Clarisse who stepped through the doorway to announce that dinner was ready. *Whew*.

Everyone stood to their feet and with further chatting and laughter, the women, except for the incapacitated Sarah, and Angelina who waited beside her, moved toward the door. She couldn't help noticing what Natalie was wearing. *Wow*. If Sarah had purchased a wardrobe calculated to snare a man, Natalie must have shopped at the upscale version of the very same store.

It left little to the imagination. Angelina thought of the concern she'd had over her low neckline, and chuckled. She had nothing to worry about. Natalie's dress was a short, asymmetrical, sequin mini in what appeared to be transparent, silver lace. The material hugged her slim figure, ending high on one tanned hip and cutting across her breasts to leave the opposite arm bare.

Angelina tore her eyes away and looked down at her cousin. The girl's face looked like a thundercloud.

As the women disappeared, Sarah hissed her annoyance. "Did you see her outfit? I suppose *she'll* be at the party, which is *fantastic* news." She sighed heavily. "I can't compete with that. I can't even walk, let alone strut around wearing nothing but plastic wrap!"

Angelina stifled a giggle. She wanted to tell her cousin it wasn't a competition, but that wouldn't have gone over well. Besides, she wasn't entirely sure it was true. There did indeed seem to be quite a rivalry for Julien's affections. She remained silent. At least Sarah's ire was directed away from her.

Julien and the grey-haired man made their way around the seating area.

"Angelina—Sarah, I would like you to meet *Monsieur* Éliott Malbec, our neighbour and friend." Julien smiled. "These are our Canadian visitors. They will be staying with us for a few weeks."

The man bowed low. "I am delighted to make your acquaintance," he said. Like his wife, and daughter, Éliott had only a trace of the accent that Julien had. Angelina wondered what part of France the Malbec family were from. "Please, feel free to visit our estate," he continued. "Although it is not the high standard you find here, you are most welcome."

"Nonsense, Éliott. Your groves are carefully tended and do you credit to them." Julien swept Sarah into his arms and lifted her easily as he turned to walk toward the dining room.

Despite the fact that she was in Julien's arms, Sarah appeared uncomfortable. "I'm sorry you have to carry me everywhere," she said. "I feel like such a pain."

Julien shook his head in denial. "You are our guest *et pas de problème*." His face creased into a grin. "Which is to say, it is not a problem. I think tomorrow we shall take a drive to the coast *ma chère*." He smiled down at her.

Sarah revived at his words. "To Marseille?"

"No, my dear," he sounded indulgent, as though speaking to an injured child. "To Cassis. It is a small fishing village on the Mediterranean coastline southeast of 'ere. During the summer it is almost impossible to visit due to crowds, but we will 'ope for the best..." he said, and shrugged. "We will go later in the day. This will help, and I know of places to park."

"It sounds lovely." Sarah's good spirits were restored, at least until Julien set her in a chair partway along the long dining table in order that he could clear out nearby seating and elevate her ankle. Once she was settled, he walked to the far end to sit beside his mother at the head of the table.

"You may take the chair to my right, next to your mother," Elyse said to Natalie. "And you, Éliott must sit beside Julien to continue your conversation." The man nodded graciously, but as he pulled out the indicated chair, his daughter slid into it and laughed up at him.

"*Merci*, Papa."

The man merely chuckled and moved to the other side. It was clear he approved of his daughter's advances upon their host.

Watching this tableau unfold, Sarah scowled. True, Angelina wasn't thrilled to see such blatant flirting either, but she had no intention of admitting that fact through a sour expression.

Clarisse directed Angelina to take the seat next to Sarah. Small talk was made, mainly by the Malbec family. Although she listened attentively, her input wasn't required so Angelina applied herself to another delicious meal prepared by the marvelous Chef Armand.

As each dish was set before them, Angelina tried to guess what ingredients had been used. First came scallops in a delectable basil sauce. Clarisse bent close to her ear and whispered.

"*Croquilles St. Jacques*. The scallops are fresh, as is all the seafood here. It is *tres bien*."

"*Merci*," Angelina whispered back and lifted a morsel of the appetizer to her mouth. It was excellent, as was the next course, but apart from knowing it was fish, and that the tiny round pellets must be capers, she had no idea what it was.

She caught Clarisse's eye as the girl brought two bottles of white wine to the table and set them down. The girl winked and murmured, "Monkfish," as she passed by on her return to the kitchen. Angelina took a bite and lifted her napkin to dab away sauce that had found its way onto her cheek.

"I notice that you have replaced your marketing manager, Julien," Natalie was saying with a pout. She set her cutlery down and placed both manicured hands on the sleeve of his jacket, pressing herself close. "I could have filled that position for you, *cheri*. Instead, you have hired some old man. Why?"

It was only because she had been savouring the food that Angelina happened to be looking across the table at that moment. She was surprised to see Julien's face darken. It was only for a moment, but she could see he was struggling with some deep emotion. His knuckles whitened as he gripped his fork.

"*Oui, c'est vrai, mais je ne veux pas en discuter maintenant.*" Julien spoke with a low, but commanding voice in rapid French. Either he was too upset to realise he had neglected to use English for the benefit of his guests, or he was hoping to hide his response. Yet, Angelina understood enough to know he'd told Natalie he had no intention of discussing it with her now.

"Are you enjoying your meal?" he asked, encompassing the entire table in his query as he smoothly changed the topic to that of praising his fabulous cook. As everyone assured him the food was delicious, Angelina lowered her eyes to her plate.

Another sore subject, she mused. There seemed to be plenty of them around this place. Yet why would the loss of one employee, and substitution of another cause such an angry reaction in their host?

Without a doubt she could understand why Julien wouldn't consider hiring the beautiful Natalie. The girl was not afraid to make her intentions known. But what did the rest of it mean?

CHAPTER 9

The rest of the meal passed without further incident and as they finished off with a cheese course and sipped a rich coffee, Angelina set her contemplations aside. Éliott Malbec was an entertaining fellow, keeping the table laughing as he told stories of the troubles he and his wife had experienced upon taking over the huge, neglected olive grove some years before.

It seemed no time at all had passed before nightfall descended and the Malbec family took their leave. Angelina had heard of, *la bise*, the French equivalent of both a handshake and a hug. However, she was unprepared when Madame Malbec embraced her and kissed each cheek with a loud smack that didn't quite touch her face. With a laugh, Angelina decided it was a gesture she found charming.

Until Natalie grasped her shoulders in a chilling clinch, that was. The young woman's eyes were like chips of ice and Angelina felt sure there was an unspoken warning in their frosty depths—*stay away from Julien.*

She almost laughed aloud and answered that the girl should have no fear of her. Yet, when she saw the same performance repeated for Sarah's benefit, Angelina was annoyed. *What right did this person have*, she thought later, as she bade her cousin goodnight and closed the door to her own room. Certainly, Julien did not appear to share Natalie's sentiments.

Her mind flicked back to relive the sensation of his lips on hers. She couldn't remember feeling that electricity with any of her previous boyfriends. But Julien wasn't a boyfriend or anything remotely close to it, she reminded herself sternly.

She opened the large French door and stepped out onto her tiny balcony, drawing the smells of a Provencal twilight into her lungs. The air was spicy with the scent of pine, herbs, and the many flowers that flourished in the garden. She grasped the railing and leaned over top, searching for a glimpse of the moon as she took a deep breath.

"Come down and walk with me." Julien stood in a ribbon of light from an open door below. He held up a beckoning hand, asking her to join him as though he were Romeo and her Juliet. Two star-crossed lovers meeting despite the wishes of their opposing families. At least, that was the wild thought that skittered across her mind as she nodded without considering the consequences and hurried downstairs to join him.

Breathless, she arrived on the patio by the pool and scanned the now empty terrace, searching for him. Her eyes caught movement and saw that he was perched on the low stone wall that ran around the perimeter of the garden. She took a deep breath, hoping to slow her pulse.

The low tones of his voice carried to her as she picked her way along the rocky path. "Some call it, *garrigue*," he said. "The scent of Provence. In French it refers to scrub brush or the low vegetation that grows on the limestone hills of the Mediterranean coast."

"Wow."

Angelina kicked herself for not saying something more original, but she was having an issue with her breathing. She could feel his eyes, watching her progress, silhouetted against the lights of the chateau.

"Shall we walk?" he asked, slipping off the wall and moving to meet her. He was far too close, she thought, his proximity working a strange magic with her senses. "Or..." he paused, and his voice grew husky. She knew he was not as unmoved as he would like her to believe. "Or shall I kiss you now beneath the light of Shakespeare's tragic moon?"

"We should walk." Angelina answered in a strangled whisper, taking a step away. How was it that he had been thinking of Shakespeare too? Mentally, she doused her racing thoughts with a jug of ice water and began to babble, asking a series of questions without giving him time to answer any of them.

"So, *garrigue* hey? That's an interesting word. How did you know I was enjoying the fragrance of the air tonight? Is there some new flower blooming now that doesn't smell during the day? I can tell there's a different scent out here." She hurried in front, not waiting for him to catch up, yet hoping perversely that he would.

It took a moment for him to reply. "There is. My mother brought the seeds back from America when she was visiting friends one summer and has tended it ever since. It is called a moon flower." Gravel crunched underfoot as he drew alongside her.

"Oh, how romantic," she said, rounding on him with delight.

"My mother always thought so. Do you wish to see them?" Angelina nodded and noticed the silvery light of the moon, rising into the sky above them. It lent an added enchantment to an already surreal stroll.

"Follow me," Julien said, taking the lead. He veered along one of the many winding paths that crisscrossed throughout the garden until he stopped in front of an area of plants that grew higher than Angelina's waist. White, trumpet-like blossoms bobbed in the slight breeze and glowed in the light from above.

"They're beautiful."

"Yes, the flowers unfurl in the evening and stay that way until sunrise," he said, matter-of-factly. His arm brushed hers as he grabbed a stem and snapped a leaf into his hand. "But the plant is deadly if ingested. We have no pets or children here. If we did, I would move the plants to a safer area."

"The scent is gorgeous," she murmured, taking another deep breath.

"Have you never been married or had kids?" she asked, in a sudden rush of words. The merest touch of his sleeve was beginning to affect her now. It had been a dangerous proposition to join him for a late-night walk.

She would be sure to avoid moments like these in future.

He gestured that she continue walking and he fell into step beside her before responding. "No, I 'ave not married. Nor do I 'ave a child. Running this estate has always consumed my free time and that was 'ow I liked it—until recently."

Angelina found that she was holding her breath. Until recently? Was he seeing someone?

He shoved his hands into his pockets and kicked at a larger rock on the trail. "No one knew," he said, expelling a long sigh. "She was my employee and I 'ave strict rules about dating on the job. But...," he shrugged, "these things 'appen sometimes. I was about to tell *ma mere* about 'er when..." He broke off. "If I 'ad obeyed my own rules the situation might 'ave been different."

They walked in silence for several moments more before he concluded his tale. "I was seeing the marketing manager Natalie spoke of this evening. Only for a short time, but I thought it was going well, until she ran away with a married man and was killed near Paris." He ran a hand through his hair.

"Oh, Julien! I'm so sorry." Angelina came to a sudden halt and placed her hand on his arm. "That's terrible. You must have been devastated."

"*Oui*," he said simply and edged away from her hand. She had the impression he'd been needing to get this painful information off his chest, but in telling it, was taken back to the remembered pain.

"I understand," she said, as they continued walking. "In the past three months I was dumped without even a word of explanation and fired from my job, because I rejected the advances of the boss' son."

It was Julien's turn to stop and although his face was just a shimmery orb in the moonlight, she could tell he sympathized.

"We are quite a pair," he said. "Is this why you came to France?"

"It's not *why* I came, but it is what allowed me the time to do so."

She wasn't about to tell Julien the real reason she had accompanied her impressionable young cousin. Thinking about it reminded her of her true purpose in being here, and it wasn't to skulk around French gardens in the dead of night, with a man she didn't trust.

"Anyway," she said, in her best schoolmarm imitation, "I should be getting back inside. It must be late."

"*Bien sûr.*" Julien raised no objection. Indeed, his voice sounded almost as formal as she had made her own.

As Angelina stepped back into the house and they wished one another a chilly good night, she felt relief that she'd dodged another bullet. Had he kissed her instead of asking if he could, she wasn't sure she would have resisted.

CHAPTER 10

The next morning dawned bright and clear. Angelina pulled her drapes and lifted her face to the sun. Her heart was light. She had plenty of time to spend a leisurely morning at the chateau before they left on their excursion to the Mediterranean that afternoon.

She pulled her hair into a high ponytail and dressed in turquoise shorts with a matching ruffled tank top. After slathering on copious amounts of sunscreen, she left her room to knock at Sarah's door. Unsurprisingly, there was no answer.

She ran downstairs, thinking of what Julien had revealed to her the night before. No wonder he'd shut Natalie down when she'd asked him about his marketing manager. It wasn't something he wanted to draw attention to or remember.

Last night's revelations answered a few of Angelina's questions. Yet, when she recalled that first evening, and what she'd overheard Julien say to whoever had been on the phone with him, she knew it still didn't add up.

Would Julien get so worked up about this betrayal as to threaten someone to keep quiet about it? She didn't think so. There was more to the story than she knew.

"Look," Sarah called excitedly, waving her over as soon as Angelina entered the kitchen. Her cousin was having a croissant and coffee at the small table in the corner of the expansive room, but slid forward on her chair to stick her injured foot in the air. She was wearing a loosely laced running shoe. "I can walk today! Well...sort of," she amended with a giggle. "I'm still limping a little, but the ankle feels much better."

"Great news." Angelina stepped closer to inspect the foot as Sarah wished. "You'll be feeling much better by tomorrow night. I trust you haven't forgotten the party." Angelina winked at her cousin. The girl laughed.

"Yes. I want to talk to you about that." Sarah lowered her voice. "Julien left you a car for us to use, right?" Angelina nodded. "Then why don't we go somewhere and buy new dresses."

Angelina pulled out a chair and plopped down in it. "I suppose we could," she agreed, thinking of her limited wardrobe. "Julien said he'd take us to Cassis today, though. Dress shopping can take a long time, especially when we don't know where we're going."

"I spent time online last night, researching the best shops and found one in particular. I have it all mapped out—if you'll go." Sarah gave her a wheedling look and Angelina reached for her hand to give it a squeeze. It was obvious her cousin was determined to purchase a dress to rival the sheer, silver sheath that Natalie had worn the evening before.

"Of course. I'll have a coffee and we'll leave."

The keys for the little lemon-coloured Citroën were on a table in the foyer. Angelina grabbed them, collected her bag, and helped Sarah hop down the steps and settle into the passenger seat.

Angelina enjoyed driving the 5-speed manual. They flew down narrow paved roads into the nearby town and thanks to Sarah's meticulous directions, arrived at a shop in record time.

In less than an hour and a half, they returned, laughing, to the car and stuffed several colourful bags into the back seat. Angelina was grateful Sarah had suggested the excursion. They'd had fun together, plus, she'd found a great dress and stilettos to wear to the party. Secretly she'd been dreading the thought of wearing a worn sundress with her old, flat sandals. Now, she was set.

In a matter of two hours, they were back at the chateau and ready to leave for their outing to Cassis.

૨.

JULIEN PARKED THE LEXUS ON THE SIDE OF A NARROW street in Cassis later that day, high above the fishing boats and beach Angelina had read about. The village spread out at her feet as she stepped from the car and stood on the pavement, mesmerized by the view. Creamy houses with rusty, red roofs poked out of the gaps between the soft green pines, cypress, and plane trees that grew up the rocky hillsides. A ridge of rugged mountains surrounded them, ending in a cliff that dropped sharply to the sea. And in the distance, the azure waters of the Mediterranean glittered under a flawless sky.

"It's lovely!" She clasped her hands together and turned to include her three companions. Sarah crawled from the spot she seemed fond of—directly behind Julien, to stretch and yawn. She'd fallen asleep on the forty-five-minute drive and hadn't seen a thing. On the other hand, Angelina drank up every field, tree, and rock she saw, committing them all to memory in lieu of the day she would leave this place.

Elyse appeared beside her and gently took her elbow. "It is beautiful *ma chère, mais* per'aps you should move off *la rue*, or a car might run you down. We don't want *two* injured girls."

Angelina looked around and realised she was still on the street. She grinned at Elyse, patted the lady's hand where it rested on her arm and shut the car door.

She stepped to the sidewalk and caught Julien staring at her. "We will 'ave a climb on our return, but the walk down to the harbour is not too far from 'ere," he said. "I 'ope you 'ave on your swimsuits? And brought towels?"

Sarah lifted a woven basket bag with another yawn. In her haste, Angelina had left hers inside the car. Sarah reached back for it and thrust it at her cousin. "I'm surprised you'd even bring a bathing suit. You don't swim, do you? Or will Julien have to save you if you go in over your head?"

Angelina felt herself colouring as she remembered the incident in the pool.

"There is more to do 'ere than play in the water," Julien said firmly. "If you are ready, please follow me."

Angelina was getting used to the formality of this man. Still, it was hard to know if it was his true nature, or if the sweet, teasing Julien was a more accurate expression of his personality. He seemed to be in deep thought today, having spoken no more than two words on the drive here.

Sarah reached for his arm as he strode toward her. He stopped and looked doubtfully at her running shoes.

"You are sure the ankle is better?" he asked. "I could drive you closer to the main area of town if you wish. I just cannot park there."

Angelina glanced at him and wondered if she imagined his lips compressing as Sarah reached out to grab hold. Was he tiring of the girl so soon? However, he took Sarah's hand as she wished.

"No. I feel perfectly fine." Sarah took a few prancing steps just to show him and pulled her sunglasses down her nose to bat long lashes. "But I do appreciate your help."

Angelina couldn't help but wonder how Sarah had made such a fast recovery, unless much of the injury had been embellished to gain the attention of their host? The image she'd seen of Julien holding Sarah for a kiss in her room that day crept unbidden into her mind as she watched the girl flirt. With a stab of something that felt like jealousy, she pushed her thoughts aside.

"That's great." Angelina urged everyone to go ahead of her. Limping ever so slightly, Sarah leaned on Julien's hand.

For Sarah's sake, Julien set a slow pace as they wound their way down to where the boats were moored, and fat palm trees stood sturdily against the sea breeze.

Angelina alternated between watching Julien's broad shoulders and lean, muscular legs, and the town as it unfolded before her eyes.

Fishing boats and pleasure crafts bobbed on the water beside a broad promenade that ran in front of the many small restaurants and shops whose doors were open to visitors. Each pastel-coloured business boasted an awning to offer their patrons some shade as they perused a wide selection of interesting items.

Julien led them past this area and along the east side of the small harbour to where pots, bulging with flowers, hung on lampposts, and a rocky beach overlooked the sparkling sea.

Sarah moved carefully down the two concrete steps leading off the walkway to the beach area beside the water. She dropped Julien's hand reluctantly and stretched.

"I'll stay here for now." Angelina straightened the brim of her hat to offer better shade from the sun and positioned herself on the top step. "Sarah's right, I can't swim and I'm afraid of water. It's okay, someone has to watch our things." She smiled convincingly at them. "Enjoy yourselves."

Without a second glance, Sarah peeled off her jean shorts and tank top to reveal a florescent orange bikini with pink flowers scattered across the tiny triangles of material that made up the suit. She adjusted a strap and looked at Julien.

"*You're* coming in with me, right?" she pleaded.

"*Bien sur.*" He smiled for the first time that day and bent to undo his leather sandals.

"I will sit for a while, as well," said Elyse as she dropped beside Angelina.

"*D'accord.*" Julien kicked off his khaki shorts and tugged his white t-shirt over his head. Angelina had to force herself to look away, particularly as his eyes met with her own and held them captive. She took a deep breath and peered along the beach, aware of Julien's footsteps in the sand as he left.

"The building on the cliff, is it very old?" She pointed, showing Elyse what she was referring to.

"*Oui.* It is a medieval chateau dating back to the 13th century." Without turning, Elyse appeared to know what Angelina was asking about. The lady crossed her legs in front of her. "It sits atop the cliffs of Cape Canaille. The scene is quite stunning, yes?"

"It certainly is." Angelina looked a moment more before directing her gaze out to the waves, searching for the familiar faces of Sarah and Julien. Finally, she spotted them bobbing up and down along with countless other people splashing in the sea.

"My 'usband loved it 'ere." Elyse spoke quietly, barely above a whisper. Her breath caught in a sob, and she scrabbled at the bottom of her bag. Finally finding a tissue, she held it to her eyes.

Angelina slipped an arm around the woman's thin shoulders and sidled closer. "If you'd like to talk about him, I'd like to listen."

"Georges and I were 'appy for thirty-seven years." Elyse began haltingly. "We raised three children and managed the family estate after 'is parents died." She raised her face to the bracing sea air and gulped. "But something 'appened to 'im. It was the beginning of

March that he became distant. I felt 'e drew away from me on purpose. I don't know why. Georges wouldn't talk things through as we used to do."

She folded and fussed with the tissue until it was reduced to shredded bits in the palm of her hand before she stuffed it back into her purse. Angelina didn't know what to say so she remained silent, allowing the woman space to think and to speak when she was ready.

"I don't know why I am telling you all this," Elyse said, then looked up with red-rimmed eyes and attempted a smile. "You didn't know 'im and barely know me." She picked up her bag and moved it restlessly to a spot between her feet.

"Sometimes it's best to talk to someone who is an outsider," Angelina said. "You can be assured I won't speak of it to anyone that you know, and I have an impartial viewpoint. Plus," she added, giving the woman a squeeze, "I may not know you too well, but I'd like to, and I care."

Elyse patted Angelina's other hand. "*Merci beaucoup*." The two women stared out to sea for a long moment and then Elyse continued. "...Georges was not affectionate any longer and began to spend long hours at work. I tried to talk about it with 'im. Tried to show 'im that whatever the problem was, we could get through it, together. But 'e was gone from me—in 'ere," she patted the spot above her heart. "And now, I will never know what was wrong."

"I'm so sorry." No wonder Elyse couldn't find closure after her husband's death, and it was unsurprising that Julien had wanted her to have a change of scenery. She was struggling to carry a great burden and there was no relief in sight. The man, Georges, was dead and their relationship issues would never be resolved.

A lump rose in Angelina's own throat. What torment this woman must be going through. It was much worse than being fired or having your boyfriend leave you. Her heart went out to Elyse and also to Julien. He had lost his father, after all.

They sat together in companionable silence until, dripping with seawater and laughing, Julien and Sarah returned for their towels. But all laughter died on Julien's lips as he looked from his mother to Angelina and then back again.

"What is wrong?" Briskly, he began rubbing himself down, his eyes imploring his mother to explain. Whatever else he might be, Julien appeared to be a good son and Angelina was glad.

"Nothing." Elyse jumped to her feet. "Don't tell me you're quitting already? I 'aven't even dipped a toe in the water."

Julien searched his mother's face for answers, but then, apparently giving up, he wrapped the towel around his hips and sat. "I for one am finished, but I believe Sarah is anxious to continue, *n'est-ce pas?*"

Sarah, who had been fishing around in her beach bag, held up a water bottle and cheered. "Sure," she said, "I'll go back in as soon as I get a drink of water that isn't pre-salted." She grinned. Angelina knew her cousin hadn't sensed the tension or sadness surrounding Elyse and her son. She was glad there would be no awkward questions posed by a nineteen-year-old girl.

Elyse removed her glasses and hat, pulled the loose, colourful shift she'd been wearing over her head, and ran like a schoolgirl down to the water to plunge into the waves.

"Wow," Sarah said, almost choking on her drink. "That lady has spunk."

Julien and Angelina laughed as Sarah tossed her bottle of water aside and sprinted after the older woman.

"Is my mother alright?" Julien asked the question the minute Sarah was out of earshot.

"Yes. She had a few tears, but she's strong. I admire her greatly."

"My father was fond of Cassis," Julien continued. "Is that what prompted her to reminisce?"

"She mentioned that, yes." Angelina wasn't sure if Julien knew of his parents' marital problems and was reluctant to say too much.

"I respect that you do not give away her confidence," he said. "It is another of your most admirable qualities. But...if she told you about the difficulties they 'ad during the last few weeks of 'is life, I assure you, I know about it all too well." His voice was harsh and angry as he finished speaking. Her head jerked around to face him.

"What is it, Julien?" she asked with concern. He stared across the heads of sunbathers, his mouth set and grim. Gulls screeched overhead, the hubbub of holiday-makers rose on the air, and the briny smell of the sea tickled her nose. Yet, all of these attractions faded away like waves upon the sand as she studied his handsome profile. An urge to reach out and touch him overwhelmed her and she extended a hand to his forearm.

He spun around and his grey eyes, searching her

own, darkened. Angelina wasn't sure how it happened, but suddenly his lips were moving against hers and a sensation of bliss like she'd never known swept over her body. Angelina's eyes drifted shut. She felt as though she were melting into him, and she leaned toward Julien, her heart on wings.

Then, rocks pelted her legs, and she broke away with a wrenching sting of pain. Was it Sarah, furious with her behavior? But throwing rocks was far too juvenile, even for her young cousin.

Hastily she looked for the source of the discomfort, turning away from Julien, but still feeling the warmth of his body pressed next to her own. She almost succumbed to the sensation, turning back to continue the kiss, but he was standing and saying something loudly in French to two small children who scampered away giggling.

"*Désolé pour ça*," he said, forgetting his English again. But she knew already that he was sorry he had kissed her, it was evident on his face that had again hardened with anger.

"It's nothing," she mumbled. "No harm done." Reaching down she dabbed at two scratches on her left leg that oozed a little blood.

"But you are hurt," he exclaimed. "It is inexcusable that these children should treat us this way. Can I 'elp you. Perhaps I 'ave *des pansements* in the car. I don't know 'ow you say it..."

"Band-Aids," she supplied. "And it's fine. They're kids. Tis only a flesh wound." She looked up at him, but her attempt to be humorous fell flat. He was still scowling.

Secretly, Angelina felt grateful to the children. What would have happened if Sarah arrived on the scene? Then the fur would have flown. She'd never have gotten off as lucky as to have only a few scrapes. She felt as though, somehow, the whole incident had been her fault. Yet she was still no wiser as to why Julien had been so upset.

"You are sure I cannot get you anything?" he asked once more. When she nodded, he dropped down beside her again, but kept distance between them this time.

The sun was slowly getting lower in the sky. It was still hot, but people around them were beginning to pack up their things and head back from whence they came. A baby cried, startling Angelina. She'd been lost in thought. What made this enigmatic man tick and what were the secrets he held so close? She pushed her sunglasses further up her nose and scanned the area for Elyse and Sarah. Soon enough they would emerge from the water and join them.

"There is something I 'ave not told my mother concerning my father's death," he said quietly. Angelina caught her breath, but stopped herself from turning toward him like before. "There are only an 'andful people who know it and I 'ave sworn them to secrecy. The information would devastate 'er and I will not allow it." His voice grew stronger.

Angelina waited in silence. It was not her business to know what this hidden information was, but she knew it hung like a pall over this family and wished there was something she could do to make it better.

A breeze picked up, and across the glittering diamond of the Mediterranean, a ship hove into view.

Angelina tipped her hat further down so she could squint. It appeared to be a huge cruise ship making its way along the beautiful Côte d'Azur with several thousand passengers on board. All at once, Angelina was filled with gratitude. To be here with this man, in this place, at this time in her life was perfect and she sighed audibly.

Julien caught her hand and turned her to face him. "You are 'appy here?" he asked.

It was a complete departure from where his mind had clearly been only moments before, but she nodded. "Yes. I'm happy Julien." Her words held a wealth of meaning, much more than he had meant, she was sure. He dropped her hand and looked toward the water's edge. Elyse and Sarah were wading out of the water and heading back for their towels.

Of course, he wouldn't want to be caught holding her hand in front of Sarah. Angelina rubbed it down the ruffles of her turquoise top and pasted a bright smile on her face as the two dripping women strode along the beach toward them.

"For the first time in a very long time, I believe I am almost 'appy too." Julien watched as his mother and Sarah walked toward them. His sentence was scarcely perceptible, and the summer breeze bore it away as quickly as it was uttered. Had he meant for Angelina to overhear him? She wasn't sure, but she stored the words away for later contemplation. It couldn't have been about her.

CHAPTER 11

Angelina stepped in front of the mirror behind the bathroom door and stared at her reflection. In her heart she admitted she was dressing for Julien, but did it matter? He had eyes only for Sarah and it was better that way. Her job was to see that Sarah returned home safe and unscathed by the wiles of this debonair Frenchman.

She was nothing more than a truck driver without fixed employment. Angelina shook herself and lifted her chin. No. She was a professional driver, and a bloody good one too. There was no time for self-pity. The party was about to begin.

Running fingers through her pride and joy; the long black hair that cascaded down her back in soft waves, her green eyes sparkled at her with a mischievous glint. No, she would not let past troubles get her down. Not tonight.

The dress she had purchased hugged the lines of her

shape perfectly, but was comfortable due to the stretchiness of the material. It dropped into a mermaid-ruffle-hem starting just above her knees and dipping low at the back of her legs. It was a deep forest green with round neckline. Another ruffle began over each shoulder and ran down to her small waist, accentuating her curves, while the back cut away leaving her skin bare. It was perfect. Not too revealing, but definitely form-fitting. With a chuckle, Angelina lifted one arm and made a muscle while looking in the mirror. All those years at her chosen occupation had left her arms toned and fit.

Pushing the door shut, she moved to the mirror over the sink to apply a muted shade of lipstick and dab some perfume behind her ears. Then, padding to her dresser, she found the earrings that had been half price in the shop, and added matching long threads of rhinestones that twinkled in her cloud of dark hair. Lastly, she perched on the edge of a chair to fasten the thin straps of her new silver, high-heeled sandals.

At last, she stood ready to take on the world, or at least the people that had been invited to the party. Taking a deep breath, she ran clammy hands down the font of her dress, then opened the door, and stepped into the hallway.

It was quiet, although the sound of laughter and low discussion floated up the broad staircase. Feeling a twinge of nervousness, Angelina stepped to Sarah's door and tapped. To her surprise the door swung wide, and a hand urged her to enter.

"I thought you'd be long gone," she said.

Sarah pushed the door closed with only a faint click to mark the latching and fell against it wearing a stricken expression and a fuzzy purple bathrobe.

"*Shhh!*" Sarah's eyes widened, if that were possible since she looked like a deer in the headlights already. She spread her arms wide in defeat. "My dress ripped, because I'm too fat! What am I going to do?" She flopped backward onto the bed and groaned.

"Let me see it," insisted Angelina. She'd worried when Sarah purchased the dress that the girl was trying to squeeze herself into something far too tight, but her cousin had been adamant that it had to be this dress. Angelina knew why, of course. Sarah felt driven to outdo the neighbour who'd appeared that night in her skin-tight, thigh-high, low-cut mini. But this wasn't going to work.

Sarah arose, picked the dress off the floor where it lay in a crumpled ball and tossed it to Angelina before throwing herself, with another hopeless groan, back across the bed. Even her curly blonde hair looked dejected.

"You look great, by the way," she said in a small, muffled voice.

Angelina bent her head to hide a smile and began to search for the tear. The dress was a gorgeous, deep blue, sequin mini that Sarah had planned to wear with impossibly high, silver stilettos. Finding the problem, she inspected it at close range.

"This isn't so bad," she said, tugging at the rest of the zipper to check for further flaws. "And don't be ridiculous, you're not fat. It wasn't you at all. A seam ripped a little, because the threads were already giving way. I could sew this up in no time if I had a needle and some thread."

"But you're horrible at sewing, aren't you?" Sarah remained face down on the bed, mumbling into the duvet. "It's hopeless. I'll just lie here and wait for old age to claim my withered corpse."

Angelina sat on the bed beside her and laughed outright. "You silly girl. I'll fetch my bag. I always bring a few safety pins, a needle, and a bit of thread when I go on a trip. Yes, I'm rotten at sewing, thank you very much. But a one-armed orangutan could throw a few stitches into a ripped seam. It's nothing."

Sarah rolled over and lifted her head. "You're sure?" When Angelina nodded, she sprang up and rushed to a mirror to examine her hair and makeup. "Okay."

Angelina slipped across the hall and found the small sewing kit at the bottom of her armoire.

In no time at all, the dress was repaired, and Sarah shimmied into it. With care, Angelina zipped it to the top and Sarah stood before the mirror to admire her reflection. She did indeed look ravishing. The sapphire sequins danced with light and life and clung to every curve. Angelina caught sight of herself beside the young girl and wondered if she looked like an old maid by comparison. Oh well, there was no point in worrying about it now.

"Are you ready?" she asked Sarah.

"Ready."

Together they descended the staircase. "Mind you don't trip and wrench your ankle again," Angelina whispered. "I can't believe you're trusting yourself to wear those things."

"It's not about practicality, cousin. It's about catching a man."

"You're nineteen. You don't need to *catch* anyone." Angelina sighed inwardly. There was no reasoning with the girl.

With a flutter of her hand, Sarah dismissed Angelina's statement. They reached the bottom step and tapped across the foyer. Then, Sarah gave her cousin an exaggerated wink, stuck a coquettish smile on her face and entered the lounge.

More than twenty people were already enjoying a glass of wine and the conviviality of the Belliveau family. Angelina heard the front door open behind her as more arrived. Somehow, she hadn't realised there would be such a crowd. She stepped into the room, her eyes searching for the familiar faces of either Elyse or Julien.

It was Elyse who hurried forward and grasped her and Sarah by a hand. She drew them into the room.

"*Excusez-moi tout le monde,*" she called, speaking loud enough that all could hear. When the room grew quiet and all eyes turned to them, she continued. "*Je voudrais présenter mes amies,* Sarah Peterson *et* Angelina Fisk." The crowd of people nodded and smiled in acknowledgement of the introduction while a few openly gaped at them with interest.

Angelina, colouring with all the attention, looked across the room to the windows and the sanctuary of the outdoors. Her heart slammed into her stomach as she locked eyes with Julien. He stood, peering over the shoulder of a man that appeared to demand all courtesy be awarded to him. Julien lifted his hand in a small gesture of apology for only Angelina to see. It was clear he could not escape the conversation, but his eyes—oh his eyes wouldn't let her go and her heart swelled.

"Why are you standing here like a statue?" Sarah hissed through gritted teeth as she struggled to maintain her grin. "Elyse asked us to join her to meet her daughter and you acted like you didn't even hear her." She pointed to the sofa where a young woman held a small child on her lap. "I need you to stay with me since you know more French than I do."

Reluctantly, Angelina tore her gaze away from the only person she wanted to speak to in the whole room. "Okay," she agreed, allowing herself to be led. By the time they wove their way through the crowd, Angelina realised Sarah needed her for more than her French. Her cousin was wobbling on her heels and leaned heavily on Angelina's arm for support. Sarah would have pitched into the full drinks tray that Clarisse stopped to offer them if Angelina hadn't hauled her back in the nick of time.

"I 'ave to say, I believe this strange inability to stand —this fondness for falling upon people and things, must run in your family." Julien's breath tickled her ear, and she felt his lips moving in her hair. Smoothly, he relieved her of Sarah's weight and took the girl's arm himself.

Even though she knew she should respond sharply to his bantering, all Angelina could do was grin. He really was a tease. And sadly, he was right. It did appear as though neither she nor her cousin could stay upright for any amount of time at all. This had never happened to her before. Involuntarily, she planted her feet wide as they stopped in front of Elyse.

Sarah must not have heard the remark as she gazed up at Julien with undisguised adoration.

"Ah, there you are," the lady said with obvious pleasure. "I would like you to meet my daughter, Lia, and my grandson Mylan." The young woman looked first at Sarah, taking note of how she clung to Julien, and then at Angelina. There was curiosity in her eyes, but not unfriendliness.

"*Enchantée*," she said. The boy hid his face on her shoulder. He couldn't have been more than three or four. Lia patted his back and smiled, her eyes lighting up. "I am so glad we could meet. I have heard so much about you both."

Lia barely had any accent at all. She was petite and slim, like her mother, and had the same chestnut-coloured hair. Only it was short and trimmed into a pixie-cut that accentuated her dark brown eyes. As her son squirmed, Angelina noticed something else; the woman was about five months pregnant.

Introductions were also made to her husband, Mathéo. He was standing behind his wife, in deep conversation with the neighbour from the night before, Éliott Malbec, who also greeted them with a polite *bonsoir*. Both men turned back to their discussion.

As Lia questioned Sarah on whether or not she was enjoying France, Angelina's eyes drank greedily at the fountain of Julien. He wore a light, navy-blue sweater that hugged his broad shoulders and was tapered to end just over the belt of snugly fitted dark grey dress pants. His shoes looked to be made of a soft chocolate-brown leather and Angelina wondered if they were Italian. She had no knowledge of what Italian shoes looked like, but she liked these. None of the men she'd dated had ever dressed so well.

Sarah remained at the center of Lia's queries, and, as Julien propped her up, he was engrossed in the discussion as well. Angelina allowed her eyes to rove over the crowd until she spotted the person she was searching for, Natalie.

Sarah would *not* be pleased.

Again, the woman was dressed to kill. A group of three young men stood admiringly around her as she moved seductively in a black mini dress that looked like fine chainmail. It hung from thin metallic straps, the deep cowl neckline dipping well below and between her breasts, and the material skimming her body in shimmering folds. No wonder she was attracting attention. It was overtly sexy, and Angelina was not impressed. However, she admitted ruefully, other women weren't Natalie's target audience.

Angelina was brought back from her reverie by a meaningful cough. Spinning around, she beheld a handsome young man with dark hair like her own, wearing an impeccable suit with the throat of his white shirt open. He wasn't much taller than her, in her spike heels. He reminded her of someone, especially around the eyes.

"*Je suis* Raphaël Belliveau," he said with a slight bow. "And you must be…" The question was left hanging.

"Angelina," she said, holding out her hand. "So, you are Elyse's other son?"

"Oui. I am the *other* son, as you say. I am 'appy to

make your acquaintance." He shook her hand with formality and looked pointedly at Sarah.

Touching her cousin's arm, Angelina won the girl's attention and Sarah swung around still clutching Julien. Her eyes widened.

"Raphaël, you are 'ome." Julien clapped the younger man on the shoulder and grinned. "I must introduce you to Angelina Fisk and Sarah Peterson."

"*Oui*, I 'ave meet the lovely Mademoiselle Fisk," Raphaël said with another flash of even white teeth. He turned to fully face Sarah. "But I am *most* pleased to make the acquaintance of *this* ravishing woman."

Anyone could see that he and Sarah were instantly attracted to one another. She dropped Julien's arm like it was a hot potato and offered both hands to his brother with a blushing smile.

"I'm beginning to feel like chopped liver in this place," Angelina muttered to herself. Julien shot her a quizzical look that told her he'd been listening. Inwardly she groaned. She didn't want to explain.

"You feel like..." he paused, knitting his brows together with incomprehension. "A plate of diced organ meat?"

Now that he was not needed as a crutch, he edged past his brother and stood with Angelina. His eyes explored hers, waiting for a reply, but she ducked her head, giggling despite her feelings of inadequacy.

She sighed when he remained silent. "It's a turn of phrase—a saying back home. It means you're insignificant and unnoticed, usually in comparison to others." She lifted her head in resignation, hair falling away from her embarrassed cheeks, and chanced a look into his face. She shrugged. "Uh...I didn't mean for anyone to hear me."

Julien moved closer. His hands lifted to wind themselves into her billowing hair and pushed it behind her neck, his fingers trailing across the soft skin of her back. He grasped her shoulders, sliding his hands over her heated flesh. An irresistible sense of rightness flooded over Angelina, and she waited for him to pull her into her arms, longing for the moment of contact as she breathed in the scent of his cologne. The room melted away and just the two of them stood there. His scent flooded over her, and his mouth curved into a smile so close that her eyes were drawn to his lips as they lowered, almost touching her own as he spoke again.

"Then allow me to say that you are the most beautiful woman in this room, and quite possibly the whole of France," he whispered huskily. "I find you captivating and desirable, in fact..." he stopped and took a tiny step back, "I am 'aving trouble not ravishing you here and now."

"Oh..." The word slipped out on a sigh of its own. She sagged a little, feeling cheated of the embrace she'd been so sure was coming. But his hands continued to burn a brand into her arms as he moved his thumbs in intoxicating circles. His eyes darkened with desire.

She saw his chest heave and felt his exhalation of breath on her face as he pulled back. At that moment, he was jostled by his brother, and with one last probing glance, his attention was torn away.

Angelina felt as though she might topple off her high, glittering stilettos. *Strange*, she thought, gathering her wits about her. Julien didn't act like a man who had been thwarted in his attempt to win Sarah. He loosened his grip, sliding his hands down Angelina's arms to entwine his fingers with hers. His eyes, filled with promise, flickered back to her.

"Julien." Someone called his name from a far corner of the room. With a final squeeze of farewell, his fingers slipped away, and he strode toward the imperious summons. Angelina wrapped her arms around her body, suddenly feeling alone. She teetered to an empty chair and sank into it, accepting a frosty glass of wine from Clarisse who continued to make her rounds. Angelina leaned back and tried to relax, watching the room full of people enjoy themselves.

None more than Sarah, she decided. The girl was positively glowing. She clung to Raphael's jacket and laughed at something he had said. Clearly, she was employing every feminine wile she knew, Angelina thought. Lifting the glass and allowing the fruity spirits to revive her, she closed her eyes. Thoughts of the past few minutes with Julien flooded her mind and she smiled involuntarily.

Sarah was led across

the room by the guiding arm of Raphaël. Angelina watched as the man treated her cousin like breakable glass. He sat her down among a group of people that seemed to be friends roughly the same age, and then went in search of drinks. Soon he was back at her side, his dark head bent beside her fair one as he listened attentively to all she had to say.

Oddly, Angelina noticed the neighbour, Éliott Malbec, observing her as the night wore on. After the fourth time they locked eyes, she twitched nervously. It was unsettling and Angelina wondered what was causing the fellow to stare at her so pointedly. She had spoken to the man's wife and to Elyse at length and had been approached by various other guests as well. But he had made no effort to speak to her; only viewed her from afar.

It was after the fifth time she caught his unfathomable gaze that she decided to go in search of Julien. Perhaps his mere presence would ward away the ill feeling she got from the neighbour. However, as she made her way through a group of people discussing the weather, her elbow was grasped from behind.

Julien?

She whirled around with a smile and then lurched back in alarm. Éliott Malbec tightened his grip and began to steer her toward the door. Angelina felt sick. Not again.

She looked vainly for Sarah, but the girl had vanished into the milling throng that now filled the huge space to capacity. Elyse was nowhere to be seen either and only the top of Julien's head was visible at the bar as he addressed a large group of people.

"*Excusez-moi monsieur!*" she said tersely as they reached the hallway. Not wishing to make a scene inside, Angelina had allowed herself to be directed. But when the man stopped, she ripped her arm away. "What do you think you're doing?"

"Simply this, my dear," Éliott sneered. "Don't think you're fooling me with your little, visitor-from-Canada act. I know a manhunt when I see one. If you want me to keep quiet about the plot you and your young friend are concocting, then...I have a way you can buy my silence that might prove satisfying for both of us." He leaned in as though to kiss her, but even in three-inch spikes she sidestepped him with ease.

"Oh?" Angelina played dumb, knowing his intentions full well. His lewd suggestion wasn't something she wanted to acknowledge. She took another step away, but the man staggered after her, grasping again for her arm and swinging her around. Too much alcohol had turned him into a lecherous fool! And a dangerous one at that.

"I'm not interested in anything you have to say." Her eyes narrowed and she enunciated slowly as though for a child to understand. "I'm not the least bit afraid of you and your filthy threats. If you don't remove your hand from my arm, you're going to lose it."

She set her teeth and prepared herself. This man wasn't backing down. He smirked. Lunging at her, his hot, reeking breath assailed her nostrils, and his face grew huge in her vision. His superior weight and strength threw her back toward the wall, but she countered with a move of her own.

Angelina leaned away and grabbed him by the material of his shirt. Using the momentum of his own attack, she pulled him toward herself and then down as she placed her foot between his legs and turned sharply to one side. The man dropped like a felled tree to the tiled floor of the foyer. His face registered such surprise that Angelina almost laughed, but then he growled with rage and dove for her legs.

He couldn't follow through on his attempt, however, because Julien had entered the scene. One minute Angelina was dealing with the situation alone, and in the next, Julien had the man by the collar of his shirt and was hauling him upright. He lifted the gasping man off his feet and nearly shook the stuffing out of him before Angelina protested.

"You should be grateful I don't knock you senseless," Julien ground out. He dragged the man's face close to his own. "We do not take kindly to anyone who treats women in this way. My sympathies go to your wife. She will always be welcome here, but if you so much as darken my door, I will thrash you. Is that understood?" He shook the man again as if to rattle some sense into his foolish brain.

Éliott licked his lips and nodded, his eyes wide with shock.

"Now get out," Julien threw the man in the direction of the door. "I will inform your family that you are not feeling well and will await them in your car."

Louis, one of the staff, glided into the room from the dining area, as though he'd been in the wings awaiting his cue. With one smooth movement he opened the door and firmly ushered the man outside before closing the door behind him and locking it.

"Wait there, *s'il te plaît,*" Julien said to Louis. "Do not allow 'im entrance into this 'ome, ever again. I will notify 'is wife and daughter. I am sure they will wish to leave."

Julien turned to Angelina who leaned against the wall feeling the repercussions of the last few minutes.

"Are you alright, *ma chère?*" He cupped her face with gentle hands. She was shocked for sure and filled with adrenalin, but Julien's solicitude caused her to now feel strangely like weeping. She drew in a deep breath and straightened her shoulders.

"I'm okay," she said in a wobbly voice. She cleared her throat. "Really. I've dealt with worse than that."

"Again, I see what a remarkable woman you are." He stepped back, allowing his hands to drop away from her face. "Is there no end to your talents, I wonder?"

She shot him a tremulous smile. "One must feel pity for Madeleine and Natalie," she added. "This cannot be the first time his wife has dealt with such infidelity."

"No. Sadly it is not." Julien's face contorted with anger. "If there is one thing I despise, it is betrayal of any sort."

Turning on his heel, he marched back into the party. Thankfully, there had been so much racket from within that no one had been aware of the altercation in the hall. Angelina wondered how Julien had known. She lifted a hand to her brow and rubbed at the furrows between her eyes, thinking that she would sneak away to her room. She had no desire to join the party again.

She'd only taken a few steps when Natalie sashayed around the corner, the picture of composed fury. Doubtless, Julien had said more than he intended. The woman spotted Angelina making for the staircase and hurried to stop her.

"Leaving so soon?" she inquired in a saccharine voice. Angelina paused with one hand on the rail. Pity rose in her heart for the wife and daughter of the foolish man. Likely, Natalie wanted to apologize for her father's behavior.

Natalie lowered her voice and dropped the sweet tone. "I'd like to leave you with a little advice, my dear

If you think you're going to snare Julien with your cute, innocent—ways…" Natalie's eyes flicked up and down Angelina's dress. "Think again. He's unattainable. I've tried and believe me, if he won't have me, he certainly won't be interested in the likes of you." Her mouth twisted into a cruel line.

"Adrienne ruined him for anyone." Her eyes narrowed. "I see by the blank expression on your face you don't even know what I'm talking about. Do you?"

Angelina was transfixed. Of course, she didn't know what this crazy woman was going on about. Bitterness and hostility were pouring from Natalie's mouth. Her face had lost its superficial beauty. It was misshapen with rage as she shoved the strap to her evening bag over her shoulder and offered the punchline her father had been unable to deliver.

"Julien and Adrianne were engaged to be married. It was against his rules to date an employee, but rules are meant to be broken, *n'est-ce pas?* Particularly by the wealthy owner of the estate." She leaned closer.

"Don't pretend you don't know Julien and his family are worth millions. My father was right about you two. I think you're here to collect on whatever you can." She glanced behind her to see if they were still alone.

"I've never known Julien to devote himself to anything other than his work. So, I imagine it was a bitter blow when he found out that Adrianne had run away with another man." Natalie allowed her words to sink in. An evil smile contorted her face as she unleashed her words of venom.

"He will never want you or any other woman now. Not since he discovered that his fiancé had run away with—his father." Natalie broke into cackling, hysterical laugher.

As Angelina raised her eyes, glazed with unshed tears, a movement caught her eye. Elyse Belliveau stood in the doorway to the salon, a party of happy people at her back and a look of stricken horror on her face.

CHAPTER 12

Angelina plodded up the stairs to her room feeling numb. She hadn't waited for the shamed Madeleine Malbec to be escorted out the door with her horrible daughter. How many other people thought she and Sarah were visiting the Chateau de Belliveau in an effort to marry the eldest son for prestige and money?

She had not responded to Natalie's accusations or her bombshell statement. Wordlessly, she'd left Natalie standing in the foyer and, with dignified bearing, had ascended the stairs, her head held high.

Once reaching the landing, Angelina slid the sandals from her feet, picked them up, tiptoed into her room, and sat on her bed. The room spun around her.

How could Georges Belliveau have been having an affair? Elyse was a wonderful woman; so caring and warm-hearted. It couldn't be true? Yet, in her heart she knew this was the awful truth Julien was struggling to keep from his grieving mother. It would be devastating news for Elyse. Not only had she and her husband been having marital problems, but to have their marriage end in such duplicity as this; with the very woman Julien had intended to marry. It was unthinkable. Now there would be no way to know the facts or to understand why. What a heartbreaking situation?

Angelina's first inclination was to pack her things and convince Sarah that they should leave for home in the morning. This family need time to process all that had happened and heal from it. It was not the time to have guests and hold parties.

Like an automaton, Angelina hung up her dress and set the shoes in the armoire. She fingered the green material before closing the door. Julien had said she was beautiful. Her heart flooded with a warm sensation that was foreign to her and then pain overtook it.

No wonder he was often emotionally withdrawn. Not only had he physically lost his father, but he'd lost any respect he might have had for the man, along with the fiancé he loved. The betrayal was twofold.

Angelina pulled on her pajamas and padded to the bathroom to brush her teeth. She performed her nightly ritual on autopilot. When someone tapped at her door, she froze.

The tap came again, and then Sarah's whispered voice urged her to open the door. The girl burst into the room and flung herself on the bed, her arms cast wide.

"Wasn't it a perfectly glorious evening? Raphaël kissed me goodnight outside my door. Just now!" She pushed herself into a sitting position with a broad grin. "He's *so* sweet. I'm in love."

"I thought you loved Julien," Angelina said dryly.

"That was a teenage crush. It wasn't real, not like

this." She sighed rapturously and flopped back again, too wrapped up in her own happiness to notice the strain on her cousin's face.

Angelina was torn. On the one hand, she wanted to escape this house with its painful memories and hurting inhabitants. She and Sarah didn't belong here at a time like this. But that would mean having to tell her cousin everything and it was plain the girl hadn't heard a word of what had happened that night. Plus, she'd just begun an exciting relationship with Raphaël. Whether or not it would last was anybody's guess, but she wouldn't want to leave.

She had known all along that Sarah wasn't really in love with Julien, but now she knew that she herself had feelings for the man. She didn't believe anyone could fall in love so quickly. It had to be just an infatuation brought on by the situation. How else could she explain the emotions she felt?

Pacing to the window, Angelina drew the drapes for the night. She didn't want to leave Julien behind, but she also couldn't see how anything between them might work. There was no point in pursuing a relationship with a grieving man who lived in a foreign country and was a millionaire to boot. As Natalie had said, what could he possibly want with her?

He was still reeling from the bitterness and anger he felt over his father and Adrianne. He wasn't ready for a new relationship. Plus, there was a world of difference between her and this faceless Adrianne. His girlfriend had most likely been gorgeous and petite; accomplished and brilliant as the marketing manager of the entire estate.

Angelina was tall and gangly, tripped over everything in sight and drove trucks for a living. There was no comparison. Inwardly, she slumped. She would disguise any feelings she had for Julien. It was a relief to know he wasn't the type of man to use an innocent girl like Sarah, but he also wasn't anyone *she* should get mixed up with either. She would force her feelings down, they would finish their holiday, and leave.

"I'm really happy you had such a good time, Sarah," she said, infusing a false brightness into her voice. Fortunately, the girl was too wrapped up in her own thoughts to pay any notice to others. "But I'm super tired. I'll see you in the morning, okay?"

"Sure." Bouncing off the bed, Sarah pirouetted across the carpet in bare feet and disappeared. Not a sound could be heard from downstairs. Presumably, the guests had left. Sarah poked her head back around the edge of the door to look at Angelina with dancing eyes. "You can have Julien now, if you want." Laughing she shut the door with a thud and was gone.

Sarah stood staring after her. If only that were true...

❧

ANGELINA WAS RELUCTANT TO GO DOWNSTAIRS THE next morning. She had no idea what would greet her. How would Elyse have taken the shocking news? Would she even leave her room? Did she and Julien blame Angelina for what had happened the night before? Of course, none of it had been her fault. Still, she felt if she hadn't been here, they would still have their friends, the Malbecs, and Elyse wouldn't have been exposed to the horrible truth. It was all a series of what if's, but she couldn't hide in her room all day.

She felt like slumping downstairs in the fluffy white bathrobe that had been provided for her and explaining her need to lie in a dark room all day due to a headache.

No, that would be cowardly. Instead, knowing it would be another hot day, she donned a pair of old jean shorts, softened by years of wear, and a lemon-yellow V-neck t-shirt with lace inserts over the shoulders.

Shutting the door with barely a click, she made her way downstairs without stopping to check if Sarah was awake. She didn't want to talk to her cousin just yet. After the previous night, Angelina knew that the staff had been given a day off and assumed that both Belliveau men would be at work. She was grateful for the solitude. Neither did she hope to run into Elyse, but that was exactly what happened as she walked into the kitchen.

The lady of the house was alone. She had just made herself an espresso and was standing at the window cradling it in her hands, wearing what appeared to be her bathrobe; a flowery, floor-length satin gown belted tightly at the waist. She stared with swollen eyes at the expansive gardens beyond until she heard Angelina enter. For a moment, both women stared at each other. Then, with a hurried movement, Elyse set her tiny cup on the counter and rushed to Angelina, enveloping her in a close embrace.

"I am so glad you are 'ere," she said, her voice catching in a sob. "What 'appened was terrible for you. I am so sorry." She pulled back and held Angelina at arm's length. "Are you alright? I wanted to come to you last night, but I was distraught myself."

Tears spilled from the older woman's eyes. Immediately Angelina's own eyes brimmed, and she hugged Elyse again.

"I'm fine," she said, finally pulling away. "It's you I'm concerned about. You overheard what Natalie told me last night, didn't you?"

"Of course," Elyse stepped back and dabbed at her eyes with a tissue from a box on the table. Clearly, she had been using several. "But it was inevitable that I should discover the truth. Julien was wrong to hide it from me."

"He was trying to protect you," Angelina said softly. Elyse gestured that they sit.

"Would you like some coffee? It is simple to prepare you a cup." When Angelina nodded, she bustled back to the machine. Moments later they were both sipping rich, hot drinks.

"*Bien sûr*. Of course, he was. He 'oped to shield me from the painful truth, but secrets such as this cannot be kept hidden forever. I knew there was more to the story even though Julien covered up the facts. The death of my 'usband near Paris and then the disappearance of Adrianne were so close together, it is a wonder I did not connect the two myself." Elyse lifted another tissue from the box and blew her nose. "I think, deep down, I suspected it, but did not want to believe. You see, 'e was supposed to be attending a conference in Paris that weekend. Alone. Georges 'ad never lied to me before. I believed 'im."

She stood and took her tissues to a waste receptacle hidden beneath the island. Angelina finished her coffee.

"Is there anything I can do to help you?" she asked. It felt wrong to leave Elyse alone at a time like this.

"No, *merci*. I will be fine. Somehow, knowing the truth has helped me to grieve the relationship that was so strong and then was not. The month before Georges died was difficult and the time since then 'as been so painful."

She smiled tremulously. "Julien told me what you did to Éliott. He said you brought 'im crashing to the ground. The thought alone brings me great pleasure." She crossed to the table and sat again, reaching out to pat Angelina's hand.

"I am so proud of you, my dear. Éliott Malbec has always been a lustful man. He will think twice before propositioning a woman again." Elyse's emotions were stretched taut, but she still managed a chuckle.

"Now," she dried her eyes one last time, "what will you and Sarah do today? I suggest an excursion to Aix-en-Provence for the market. I will even go with you if you like. It is Saturday and still early enough that we will see much. Parking may be difficult, but I 'ave friends. They will allow us to leave the car at their house, *pas de problème*."

"Elyse, I've been thinking," Angelina clasped her hands on her lap. How should she say this? Best just to be blunt. "I feel as though Sarah and I should not be here. It's an extra burden for you and Julien to feel you must entertain us each day. I mean, you're grieving, and we aren't family." She searched this woman's face who, although she hadn't known her for very long, had come to mean so much.

"Nonsense! This 'elps me to have purpose in my life. I enjoy 'aving you girls with me. When you go 'ome I shall miss you terribly."

Elyse rose from her chair and clapped her hands together. "I will hear no more of it. Please, tell Sarah to be ready in 'alf an hour. We will find something to eat for breakfast once we are there. We are going and I will not listen to any further arguments. Chop, chop as you say."

Angelina carried her cup to the sink. "Alright, I won't argue with you any further. But please let me know if I can help you in any way, even if it's by giving you some space."

"*D'accord*," said Elyse. "Now go."

What a resilient woman. Angelina hurried from the room thinking about Elyse. She wasn't sure she could handle such news with half as much strength. Dashing up the stairs, Angelina hurried to Sarah's door. It opened at her knock and her cousin stood there, ready for the day. She looked as though she'd taken extra care with her appearance and Angelina thought of Raphaël. If they were going out, would he want to come too?

Angelina outlined the plan and Sarah supplied the answer to the question herself.

"Raphaël already texted me this morning," she said, "Several times actually." A rosy glow stole up her cheeks. "He and Julien are busy. There's been an issue to take care of with their business that will tie them up all day, so I'm quite free to go out!" Sarah already had a purse slung over one arm as though expecting this outing.

Angelina felt both relieved at not having to face Julien yet, and sad that she wouldn't see him before they left for the day.

She paused at her room to grab her bag. A fistful of euros was burning a hole in her purse where she'd stashed them after stopping at an ATM in the Marseille Airport. It was time to spend some of her cash and she knew where she wanted to start—lunch for Elyse and Sarah.

❧

Smoothly, Angelina shifted gears as they joined traffic on the busy double-lane highway. She had been surprised to learn that Elyse didn't drive. The lady sat in the front seat issuing directions. This would explain why Julien had asked Angelina if she was capable.

"Georges and I went everywhere together," Elyse explained. "There was no need for me to have a license as I had little desire to leave my home. Everything I had ever wanted was there." It was a poignant statement. Elyse followed it with a sigh as she swung her head to look out the window and dab at her eyes. She took a deep breath and stiffened her spine. "But I will not dwell on thoughts of the past. We will enjoy this day together, us girls." She used both hands to smack her thighs and end her train of thought.

The road near the Belliveau estate was not wide and there was no shoulder to speak of for the first leg of the journey. However, as they drew closer to Aix, the highway broadened, finally becoming a four-lane motorway. Angelina picked up speed.

"It isn't far, you said?" she asked.

"Forty minutes at the most." Elyse looked around her seat at Sarah who was lost in another world. "Are you quite comfortable, my dear?"

"Perfectly," Sarah answered. There was a dreamy note to her voice. No doubt she was envisioning her budding relationship with the younger Belliveau son. Although Angelina had seen the girl have crushes before, Angelina had to admit that Sarah did appear to have hit the mark this time. Raphaël appeared to be just as smitten with her.

Angelina pried her thoughts away from the subject of burgeoning love as they whizzed past vast areas of wild trees—along with olive groves and vineyards. There were as many fields of olive trees and grape vines here, as there were huge areas dedicated to wheat and canola back home on the prairies. It was refreshingly different, she decided. *I could live here.*

She shook her head to clear her mind of such foolish thinking and gripped the steering wheel tighter. Soon, the highway turned into six lanes of traffic and grew busier, but the scenery remained the same. The rolling hills were often rocky with the white limestone prevalent in this area of the world and the ever-present clear, blue sky.

Before long, they were pulling into city limits. Angelina listened carefully to Elyse as she directed their route and they soon pulled up to the home of their host's friends.

It took almost as long to walk to the market from their house, as it did to drive to the city of Aix-en-Provence, but she was glad for an opportunity to get some exercise. As they stepped along the lovely old sidewalks beside cobblestone lanes, Angelina took in the tall rows of houses all inter-connected in shades of either cream or light ginger. Flowers, particularly hydrangeas, grew in boxes and pots all adding a profusion of colour to the picturesque town.

As they walked, Elyse chatted about the weather, her friends that lived in this beautiful city, and what fresh produce Armand had asked them to pick up for him. Before long, they arrived at Place Richelme in the old centre of Aix-en-Provence. It was filled to bursting with stalls. As far as Angelina could tell, in Provence, each stall was covered with an awning to protect the sellers and their wares from the sun, not the rain.

There were long tables covered with bowls of olives, colourful herbs, and spices such as curry, cayenne, red and black peppercorns, caraway, and herb de Provence. Bunches of dried red peppers and bulbous heads of garlic were threaded onto strings and hung from the rails that held the awnings.

Every shape and variety of crusty bread and flakey pastry tantalized them near huge offerings of cheeses and meats made by friendly artisans standing ready to sell. There were bricks of pastel soaps, handmade pottery, wicker baskets, jewelry, leather goods, and art all sold by eager vendors. And everywhere was the ubiquitous presence of lavender. Angelina breathed deep and gazed rapturously at each booth. But first they needed to eat.

Elyse knew where she was going and led them unerringly through the crowd to the door of a quaint little café on the square. They chose a table outdoors, under a huge umbrella and the branches of a leafy plane tree. Angelina drew up her chair beside the massive trunk and stared at the fascinating bark. It reminded her of a camouflage jacket she had once owned. The outer, dark-coloured bark had peeled off in patches to leave the creamy insides exposed.

A waiter arrived promptly, and Elyse addressed him in French. When he had gone, Elyse explained.

"I 'ave taken the liberty to order us a selection of pastries, some butter, jam, and *café au lait*," she said. "Le petit *déjeune*r, or breakfast, is not an 'eavy meal in France. We keep it light." She gestured with a wide sweep of her arm to their surroundings. "It is an interesting place, yes?"

"Very interesting," Sarah said. "I'm headed to the jewelry first, if that's okay?" She smiled at Elyse.

"*Bien sûr*, of course," the lady said with her characteristic shrug. Today, Elyse wore a lightly patterned, pink dress that flattered her slim, youthful figure and leaned back in her chair to enjoy the view. "I think we should eat and then explore, looking at the stalls that please us for two hours and meet back here at say..." she consulted her watch, "twelve-thirty. She looked at them expectantly. "It will be lunchtime and there is a very good bistro I would like to take you to."

"That sounds wonderful." Angelina felt the familiar bubble of happiness rise in her chest. Yes, last night hadn't been a success, and a shadow hung over these people's lives, but the truth had now been exposed and healing had begun. It was a new day and life was good. She breathed deeply and drank in the sights and sounds of the market.

Merchants leaned over their tables offering samples of their wares, their faces red from hard work under a hot sun, but their dispositions remaining cheery and welcoming. Throngs of people shuffled past, some buying and some gaping at all there was to see. Children laughed and played among the legs of the visitors and dogs barked from leashes held by loving owners. And above it all the sun beat relentlessly down, baking buyers and sellers alike in its heat.

A tray of pastries, including croissants, brioche, and sliced baguette arrived along with tiny cups of frothy coffee and the best strawberry jam Angelina had ever tasted. She spooned it onto her crisp baguette, as it would never have spread. Plump berries oozed flavour and she sank her teeth in, meeting Sarah's eyes overtop. The girl was doing likewise, and they nodded at one another in appreciation.

After their quick meal they split up and each went her own way, melting into the crowd in search of treasures.

Angelina bought a sachet of lavender, a small bag of herb de Provence, and some rose-scented soap before heading back to meet the others. Sarah wasn't hard to spot in her short, white, lacy dress and wide-brimmed straw hat. She stood next to Elyse who waved.

After enjoying a languorous lunch and having the fun of showing one another their purchases, Elyse declared it was time to leave. Lazily, they strolled back to the car and set all their bags, apart from the fresh vegetables Elyse had secured for Armand, into the tiny trunk of the Citroen. The drive back to the estate was fabulous. Angelina had never appreciated air-conditioning before as she did on that day. It cooled their heated flesh, and they sank into their own thoughts for a blissful forty-minute ride back to the chateau.

THE NEXT WEEK PROGRESSED IN MUCH THE SAME manner. The three women often went out during the day for short excursions. One afternoon they toured an orchard and brought home plump nectarines, plums, and delicate pears to leave in the talented hands of Chef Armand.

Another day they strolled through the picturesque port of L'Estaque and enjoyed lunch in one of the fabulous seafood restaurants along the waterfront. Although Elyse explained it was still part of Marseille, L'Estaque had the feel of a village. Its pretty harbour overflowed with boats, their masts sticking up like toothpicks from where they bobbed on the water.

Grand villas were sprinkled between red-roofed houses up the steep slopes leading to the chalky Chaîne de L'Estaque hills, and along the seaside, tiny cobble-stoned streets were lined with shops and bars.

Angelina barely saw Julien at all. She wondered if maybe that was always how work was for him. Or perhaps he was avoiding her. Julien joined their group only occasionally for an evening meal, always excusing himself soon afterward to return to work. Sometimes she would catch him staring at her across the dining table, but he would quickly look away.

She watched as Sarah and Raphaël became closer each day. Of course, he worked on the estate with

Julien, but seemed to find plenty of time to spend with Sarah in the mornings and evenings. They went on dates to visit famous sights and ate out several times, but mostly they wandered through the gardens or sat talking and laughing by the pool.

Angelina didn't feel the same concerns about Raphaël, as she had about Julien. After asking Elyse, she'd learned he was twenty-two, not much older than Sarah, and always left her cousin at her door with a romantic farewell. Not that Angelina was listening, but it was hard not to hear the giggling on Sarah's part.

She was glad to see her cousin so happy. The ache that gnawed at her own heart, she shoved down where it wouldn't cause her undue discomfort. If she wasn't alone with Julien before she left, it was for the best. No good could come of them talking anyway.

She'd only ran into him once all week. It had been the evening of their market excursion and she had literally bumped into him as he strode around the corner of the dining room, heading toward the kitchen. He'd been startled to see her, and she got the feeling he was disappointed he had. Julien reached out to steady her. His hands on her arms caused her skin to tingle with awareness.

"*Bonsoir.*" His voice sounded clipped and formal. He stopped in front of her and there was an awkward pause. She had expected him to make a joke about her bumping into him again, but he had said nothing.

Looking into his eyes Angelina had found it hard to believe that only the night before he'd whispered into her ear how beautiful she was.

"*Bonsoir*,' she parroted back. "Is everything okay with your business? I heard there was some trouble."

He waved a dismissive hand. "It is nothing. One of our best drivers walked off the job this morning. He is somehow related to the Malbecs. I suppose 'e 'eard about last night and decided to search for greener pastures elsewhere. That is a saying you have, yes?" A faint, uncomfortable smile touched his lips.

"Yes, it's a saying." She looked earnestly at him. "But will you find other people to work? Do you need help?"

His eyes opened wide. "Are you offering?

"I am, actually."

His eyes grew wider still. "No. Raphaël, although not accustomed to the large vehicle, will take the man's place and drive. I do not require your...'elp." The long space between his words spoke volumes. *Aha, he didn't believe her capable of such a job and had dismissed her based on appearance only. Typical.* She'd dealt with this attitude all the time back home and was sick of it.

She raised both hands in the air and backed away. "Fine with me. I won't offer again."

"It is not that I doubt what you say," Julien hastened to repair the damage his words had inflicted. "As I 'ave told you before, I think you are a remarkable woman, and you 'ave many talents, it is just that..." His voice trailed off and he rubbed the back of his neck, head bowed, clearly searching for a way to change the subject. He straightened and Angelina could sense that the subject was closed. His mind was elsewhere.

"I'm glad we 'ave a chance to speak. I wanted to tell you 'ow sorry I am about last night. My mother told me long ago that Malbec was a fool, but I gave 'im the benefit of the doubt. I was wrong to invite 'im and subject you to such treatment. I apologize."

"It wasn't your fault." Angelina found herself giving him an expressive shrug, just like Elyse always did. "Although, I appreciated that you threw him out." She smiled.

Julien didn't respond. His eyes held hers solemnly as he continued to speak. "Also, I wished to say, 'ow impressed I was with your defensive skills." A reluctant grin lit up his face. "I can still see him flying through the air as you took 'old and flipped 'im on his derriere. It did my 'eart good, I can tell you."

She grinned back at him. "I've had to deal with a few idiots in the past. Especially in my workplace."

Oh?" He looked questioningly at her, but at that moment Sarah ran down the staircase. *Thank goodness.* Angelina did not want to launch into her job description, especially after he'd turned down her offer to fill in for a missing driver. He could think what he wanted.

She caught her cousin by the arm, meaning to walk with her for a moment and ask if she'd heard from anyone back home. Julien was distracted and with a quick goodbye, he left.

CHAPTER 13

On days that they stayed at the chateau, Angelina spent time wandering through the olive groves and vineyards taking pictures or just enjoying the scenery. She was getting used to the heat, although she avoided the extremes of mid-afternoon. Armed with sunscreen, a good hat, and her sunglasses, she felt ready to go anywhere she pleased for the rest of the day.

During the hours of greatest warmth, she sat in the lounge or out on the terrace reading her book and visiting with Elyse. Sometimes she was allowed in the kitchen to watch Armand cook. Those were special treats for her, although he didn't have any elaborate suppers to prepare now. The dinner party idea had fallen rather flat.

On the morning of the twelfth day, Angelina studied her reflection in the long mirror. Tomorrow afternoon she and Sarah would fly to Paris and spend time in the great city of lights before boarding an early morning flight for home. She would enjoy this last day in Provence to its fullest.

She brushed her long black hair until it shone and took care with her makeup, ending with a bright fuchsia lipstick in opposition to her feelings of melancholy. She would miss Provence, its people, and this place, very much.

She turned off the light and walked to her closet to pull out jean shorts and a flowy, cold-shoulder top, edged with pearls, and tied at each elbow. The mottled turquoise, sky blue and golden yellow paisley pattern suited her, she thought with satisfaction as she pushed her hair away from her neck to tie the drawstring neck. But she would likely see no one to admire it anyway. Her thoughts shifted to Julien. Tossing her head to eradicate the thought, she slipped into her simple, gold sandals and left, closing the door behind her with a sigh of regret. The idyllic visit was almost over.

What would she return to in Canada, without a job or anyone special in her life? Her parents and Marcie would be glad to see her, of course, and that was great. Yet somehow it wasn't the same. Again, a vision of Julien found its way into her brain. She huffed, frustrated with herself, and flew downstairs as though to leave her wayward thoughts behind.

She entered the kitchen where Elyse was already seated with a coffee at the small table beneath the floating staircase.

"*Salut* Angelina," she called brightly. "Come and sit with me. I want to share with you a marvelous idea Julien, Armand and I 'ave 'ad."

Angelina went to her friend, for that is what she

now considered Elyse, and gave her a quick hug before seating herself and clasping her hands before her on the table. The woman was radiant in a sunshine yellow dress with full skirt and a sleeveless, fitted bodice with a round neckline. Her shoulder-length, chestnut hair was done up on her head to help her stay cool throughout the day, and tiny gold hearts twinkled from her ears. Angelina would never ask how old Elyse was, but today she looked no more than forty-eight.

Armand was quick to place the usual *café au lait* in front of Angelina and she smiled her thanks. He really was a good-looking older man. Tall, with a full head of short greying hair, a moustache that twirled ever-so-slightly up at the corners, and a mouth that always seemed to be smiling, he had ruled the Belliveau family kitchen for the past five years. Angelina had been informed of this fact only yesterday. He employed the use of that warm smile now as he folded his arms and stood beside her, waiting for Elyse's pronouncement.

"We 'ave decided that we..." she said before pausing as she waved an encompassing arm, "all of us, will dine in Marseille this evening. Eating out is quite a rare occurrence for Armand as he is always the one preparing the meal, but there is a new restaurant in Marseille and 'e knows the chef. They trained together in Paris."

"That sounds wonderful." Angelina took a sip of the strong coffee and leaned back in her chair. "And how exciting to meet up with an old acquaintance."

Armand nodded and said, "I 'ave not seen Marguerite in thirty years, but I 'ear she is *magnifique* at 'er craft. I would very much like to take you all to sample her cooking." He bustled away.

"I 'ave informed my sons and...although Julien seems to think he must spend all 'is time at work of late, he 'as agreed to go." She sobered and continued. "Besides, it is your last night 'ere and I want to make it special. I will miss you girls."

Angelina looked down, blinking away the tears that suddenly sprang to her eyes. It had not been necessary for her to come on this trip. Sarah hadn't needed a chaperone, but she was so grateful that she'd set her reservations aside and joined her cousin. It was the best trip she'd ever had. Ultimately, these were lovely people and she had grown fond of them all—especially Julien.

She gave Elyse a wobbly smile. "Thank you. You have been so kind. I'll miss you too."

Elyse patted Angelina's hand where it rested on her cup and looked to Armand who was returning with a plate of hot croissants, fresh from the oven.

"Merci, Armand," Elyse said, sniffing appreciatively. She took one and crunched into it, rolling her eyes with enjoyment. Angelina took a deep breath and chose a light-as-air pastry to lift to her mouth. It was so buttery and delicious she decided to have two, so she could remember them better when she returned to the prairies of Saskatchewan.

THE DAY PASSED UNEVENTFULLY. ANGELINA PACKED the clothes she wouldn't be needing and straightened her room before stopping next door to check on her cousin. Sarah was thrilled to be going to a fancy restaurant for their last night. Yet Angelina also sensed a sadness about the girl as she prepared to spend the day pampering herself in readiness for their evening out. She didn't pry into what plans, if any, that Sarah and Raphaël had made for future contact. Now with knowing what a sensible young man he was, she didn't worry.

Instead of hanging around the house, Angelina armed herself with her usual protection against the unforgiving rays of the sun, and went for a walk. The cicadas were in full voice as she strolled through the garden. Occasionally she'd lift the bright, bobbing head of a flower to her nose to revel in its perfume. She took pictures of everything, so that no memory would be forgotten.

Circling the chateau, she came again to the mysterious moon flower. She stopped. Her mind flooded with emotion as recollections of that scented night surfaced. Her face became hotter than the sun had ever turned it when she remembered Julien asking if he should kiss her, and her nervous reaction. She'd answer differently if he asked her now, but it was best that he didn't. No man had ever come so close to her heart before. Maybe it would have been worth taking a chance on love as Sarah had done. But it was far too late now, and likely for the best.

The heart-shaped leaves of the plant provided a dense cover for the long, protruding stems of the closed flowers. They almost looked dead. But Angelina knew that come nightfall, when the breeze whispered through the garden, they would unfurl their milky-white petals and blossom for only the moon to see. How romantic.

Much longer in Provence and I'd become a poet, Angelina thought laughingly. She continued across the lawn and eventually found herself wandering along the road down to where the rich olive oils and fruity, *vin rosé* were sold to an approving public.

She entered the door and waved to the same young man that had helped her with directions after her tour of the plant. He stood behind the counter ringing up three bottles of wine for a couple in wide-brimmed straw hats. It struck her that she would like to take a sample of each wine and olive oil home with her. It would be possible now since she had purchased a rolling suitcase from a shop in L'Estaque. She traced a finger along a glistening row of pink-tinged wine, admiring the trademark label that announced the vineyards of the Belliveau family and lifted one from the shelf.

Tucking it under her arm, she moved to where bottles of olive oil lined the wall. She chose one and held it up to a shaft of sunlight that peeked through the door as the patrons left. Squinting at it, she wondered why the bottle was so dark when the wine bottles were clear.

"May I 'elp you?" She jumped, almost dropping the wine from under her arm and turned to face Julien.

My goodness, the man was gorgeous. Her mouth went dry. He was dressed more formally than usual in grey trousers and a matching jacket, leather shoes, and underneath, a black button-up shirt, undone at the neck. His deep blue-grey eyes searched hers, waiting for an answer and impatiently he pushed a lock of hair from his forehead.

She licked her lips. "I—I was just going to buy some to take home with me. We leave tomorrow," she said. They'd spoken so little over the last week that she wasn't sure he even knew.

"I am well aware of that," he said brusquely. "But I will not allow you to pay for either of these." He opened the palm of his hand and looked at her with meaning. "Please?" he asked. She handed the bottles of wine and olive oil over without a word.

"This is my little gift to you," he said with a quick flick of a smile that didn't reach his eyes. "And the oil. Is there something wrong with it?" He raised the bottle to examine it.

"Oh," she grimaced, trying to remember what the heck she'd been doing before he came. "Right, I was wondering why the oil is in a coloured bottle?"

"Ahh," he said. "The darkness keeps out the light, you understand. Sunlight degrades the quality of the oil, and it spoils faster. The great author, Homer, called olive oil 'liquid gold.' We must preserve it in that condition for as long as possible."

She giggled, and immediately kicked herself for sounding so nervous, "Understood, and thank you. I accept your generous gift. I'll save the wine for some frosty night when the temperature plummets below forty Celsius and I'm snuggled under a cozy blanket in my apartment." She grinned at him hoping to elicit a similar response.

Instead, his mouth thinned into a straight line. "You 'ave no 'ouse?"

"An 'ouse?" she repeated his word to herself, her brow furrowing as she tried to come up with what in the world he was talking about. His toe began to tap before it snapped in her brain.

"Oh! A *house*," she grinned again. "No, I have no house. It's just me and four tiny walls. But it's enough," she added quickly, seeing the lines around his mouth tighten. What was the man getting at anyway?

"I see," he said frostily. "Please, follow me and I will 'ave these wrapped for you to pack safely. It is getting late, and I am sure you want plenty of time to prepare for tonight, *n'est-ce pas?*"

"Yes." She had answered with what he seemed to want to hear, but she was unsure of what internal struggle was happening within the man. One minute he was kissing her and the next he was like a block of ice. She gathered herself together and followed him to the till where he explained, in French, what he wanted. She kept telling herself she was grateful they hadn't seen one another much before she left. Hiding her own inner turmoil, she thanked him, and waited for the bottles to be covered in bubble-wrap.

"*À bientôt*," he said, running fingers through his hair again. "I 'ave an important meeting to attend now, if you will please excuse me." Without waiting for her reply, he turned on his heel and disappeared through swinging doors into a back room.

Well, that was strange. She accepted the bag from the clerk and thanked him before retracing her steps back to the chateau. Julien had almost seemed annoyed with her, but she couldn't think for what.

In any case, it was now mid-afternoon. Although

dinner was never an early affair in the south of France, she thought she might just retire to her room and take advantage of that huge tub for once in her life.

🐌

She must have fallen asleep! Submerged up to her nose in the bathtub, she spluttered, sucked in a mouthful of the lavender-scented water, and splashed and thrashed her arms and legs to right herself. She shivered. The water was ice cold.

Pulling herself upright she pulled the plug and tiptoed across the room to the free-standing glass shower stall and stepped inside, flipping on the warm water to wash her hair and melt the ice from her veins.

As Angelina squeezed shampoo into her hand and applied it to her long locks, she reflected on her dresses. She didn't want to wear the same thing as that fateful night she'd tussled with that horrid neighbour, Éliott. Yet, nothing else she'd brought was suitable for the sort of establishment they were going.

She rinsed, added conditioner, worked it in, and rinsed again. Reaching for her towel, she clambered out, wrapped her hair in a towel, and dried herself off before shrugging into the fluffy white bathrobe to perch on the edge of her bed and consider the problem. There wasn't a choice, she decided.

Hopping off her bed, Angelina walked to the beautiful armoire to remove the emerald, green garment and inspect it for wrinkles. It would do. She reached for her shoes before padding back to lay the items on her bed.

As she passed the door on her way to do her makeup in the bathroom mirror, she heard a knock.

"Hi." Sarah didn't wait for Angelina to answer, but pushed inside before closing the door with a soft click. "I just wanted to see what dress you are choosing for tonight."

She wore a short, pink-satin bathrobe and her hair was wet and slicked to her head. Sarah leaned on the bathroom door for a moment but soon disappeared around the corner. Angelina could hear the soft plop as her cousin settled herself on the bed. Hurrying around the corner, she saw that her cousin had avoided the high-heeled sandals, but had flung herself squarely on top of the green dress. She twisted to prop her head on a hand and grinned.

"Sarah! You're sitting on the only outfit I have. Get off!"

"Oops." The girl rolled away, but the dress stuck to her as she slid to the floor. Angelina plucked the mangled dress up where it had landed and shook it, but there was no use, it was now a wrinkled mess.

She turned panic-stricken eyes to Sarah who laughed. "You should see yourself," the girl chortled. "What are you so worried about? Just pick another one."

"I don't *have* another one," Angelina ground out between clenched teeth. If ever she'd felt like wringing the girl's neck, it was now.

"Oh..." At least Sarah had the sense to be abashed. "Sorry. Why don't you borrow one of mine then? I have plenty." She flung both arms around Angelina's waist.

"Please forgive me. I'm so happy and don't want to be yelled at right now."

Angelina shook her head and extricated herself from Sarah's embrace before walking across the room to toss the dress over her one chair. "I have no intention of yelling at you. But I don't know what I'm going to do now. You're smaller than I am. I won't fit in anything you have." She lifted her arms in a gesture of resignation and then dropped them to her sides. She felt oddly like Cinderella. *Where was her fairy godmother now?*

"You will," Sarah announced. She clapped her hands together with joy. "Follow me."

Together they tiptoed across the corridor and ducked into Sarah's open doorway. Angelina's feet twisted in some clothing, and she pitched forward in the semi-darkness of Sarah's room. She caught herself by catching the corner of a dresser. Unfortunately, she'd also plunged her hand into a bowl of dried out food that Sarah had obviously been snacking on.

"Yuck! What in the world..."

"Oh, that's nothing. Just some old pasta. I was hungry during the night," Sarah explained with the flippant air of one who never cleans up after herself. "Now, let's see, I know the dress I'm thinking of is here somewhere."

As her eyes adjusted to the light, Angelina could make out Sarah crawling on her hands and knees scrabbling through mounds of discarded clothing on the floor.

"You're getting me an evening gown from a tangled mess on the carpet?" Angelina felt her head swimming.

How could this possibly be any better than what she had? "Wouldn't it help if you had some light?"

"I suppose," came the muffled reply. Then, a moment later, "Nope, don't need it. I've found what I was looking for." Triumphantly she waved a garment in the air like she was raising a white flag to herald a truce.

With careful steps, Angelina crossed to the light switch and turned it on. Sarah had scrambled to her feet by this time and waded through wads of clothing to thrust something red into Angelina's hand. Slowly she spread it out and held it up by the top. It was stunning.

"Why would you bring this here?" Angelina asked in wonder. "And how? It must weigh a ton."

"I didn't. I bought it when we went shopping that day. I didn't show you because I thought you might scold me for my extravagance. But it's not wrinkled, it's stretchy, and it *is* perfect, isn't it?" Sarah's hair was drying at right angles to her head, and she peered at Angelina with hopeful blue eyes. As Angelina gazed at her she could see the little girl of ten who'd looked beseechingly at her when asking forgiveness for breaking a dish during Christmas dinner.

"Yes," Angelina answered with a smile. She leaned forward and held the younger woman tight. "It's absolute perfection and my new heels will work too. Thank you, sweetheart."

In a little over an hour, Angelina stood on the tiny balcony of her room, breathing in the evening air. All was still. The sweet perfume of the moon flowers wafted up to her, borne by her own desire to drink in their scent one last time. She closed her eyes and let their fragrance wash over her. At this moment, everything was right with the world, and she would remember it always.

With a swish of her long gown, she turned, and lifting the hem, stepped into her room and took one last look in the full-length mirror, just to ensure everything was perfect.

She stared at the gown, knowing she couldn't have chosen anything more beautiful to wear if she had taken a week to shop for it herself. It was an ankle-length, shimmering, sequin, cherry-red sheath with a long slit over one thigh and crystal beaded straps that crossed between her shoulder blades. The back plunged to a spot below her waist, but the V-neck wasn't too low. It only accentuated her beautiful skin and soft cleavage.

Angelina raised a hand to the long dark curls that tumbled over her shoulders and flipped them behind her. *No ponytail tonight*, she thought with a wry grin. The rhinestone earrings she'd worn sparkled with the sudden flurry of movement, and her ruby-red lips made the look outstanding.

She picked up a small black clutch that Sarah had also lent her, slipped her lipstick and cell phone inside, and drew a deep breath before opening the door to her room. The hallway was empty, and she heard Sarah's tinkling laugh from downstairs. Presumably, they were all in the foyer waiting for her. She started to hurry and then forced herself to walk slowly. This was not the time to topple headfirst down the staircase and collapse in a rumpled pile at the bottom.

She saw Julien before he saw her. He leaned nonchalantly at the bottom of the stairs, looking handsome as usual in a dark suit with the addition of a patterned tie in mottled shades of reds and blacks. Her heart pounded in her ears. She steadied herself and continued walking.

Julien laughed at something Sarah said, but as his peripheral vision caught sight of Angelina slowly making her way toward him, he stepped back. His eyes grew wide as they swept over her from head to toe, lingering on the long length of her tanned leg. Their eyes locked.

He held out a hand to her as she neared the bottom and as her heels clicked onto the tiled floor, he grasped her polished fingers in his own and drew her so close that their bodies almost touched. The room swam around her. No one else existed in the world. Slowly, he twirled her for all to admire her beauty, his eyes never leaving her.

"*Tu est la plus belle femme au monde*," he whispered into her ear. Her heart sang. Julien thought her to be the most beautiful woman in the world. He released her as Elyse stepped to her side.

"*Ma chère*, you and Sarah are too beautiful to take out of the chateau! Armand," she waved a laughing hand toward him. "Please, find the gardener's rake or a broom from your kitchen to beat off the men who will surely try to steal our girls."

Everyone laughed and the spell was broken, but Angelina stored the moment away in a secret chamber of her heart. One more golden gem to add to her collection from this trip.

Armand, also outfitted in a dark charcoal suit, opened the door with a flourish and offered the lady of the house his arm to descend the stairs. Elyse had also outdone herself for the evening. She was stunning in her long black evening gown, encrusted with jewels across the form-fitting bodice. Pearls like luminescent teardrops, dangled from her ears and her hair was swept up into a chignon at the nape of her neck. But her eyes were still haunting and sad. Angelina wished fervently there were answers to the woman's questions.

Sarah and Raphaël were next. His dark good looks complimented Sarah's fair hair and skin as she was once again, 'pretty in pink.' This dress was a departure from the skin-tight outfits she'd worn in the past. It was short, but had a full, bouncy skirt. A twinkling rhinestone belt cinched in her tiny waist, while the sweetheart neckline accentuated the creamy lines of her throat.

Raphaël, on the other hand, although not as good-looking as his brother, in Angelina's opinion, was also resplendent in a black suit. His tie was patterned in shades of blue.

Cars awaited them on the driveway below—three of them. It hadn't occurred to Angelina that they wouldn't all fit in the Lexus. But when Sarah and Raphaël piled into one and purred away, and then Elyse was helped into the front seat of a car she presumed belonged to Armand, she could only assume she was supposed to ride with Julien. Could that be right?

She felt his hand at her elbow as he walked her down the steps. "I am taking my own car this evening since I 'ave some business to attend to before we leave for Marseille. You will ride with my mother if that is alright?"

"Yes," she said, trying to hide her disappointment. "That's just fine."

"I will see you all at the restaurant," he said before climbing into his car and drove away.

Once Elyse was inside Armand's car, he closed the door and quickly swivelled around to assist Angelina.

"*Merci* Armand," she said, climbing hastily inside and feeling like the air had escaped from her balloon. She arranged her gown and told herself it didn't matter. Why would she want to ride alone with Julien? They had nothing to talk about or anything in common. He was just like all the other men she'd met who hadn't deemed her worthy.

She stared out the window into the gathering dim of the night. She was leaving the very next day anyhow. *Did she care what Julien Belliveau thought? Not one bit.*

CHAPTER 14

The drive into Marseille wasn't without charm—even for a woman huddled alone in the back seat of a speeding car—staring into the obscurity of a Provencal sunset. The lights of the city twinkled against the undulating waves of the Mediterranean Sea as they wound their way through the streets and closer to the water.

When they finally pulled into a parking lot, Angelina felt better. She resolved to enjoy the evening for what it was—a fabulous outing at a restaurant so far beyond her means that it would be the experience of a lifetime, with good friends she was never likely to see again. It sounded strange when she thought of it like that, and her eyes rested on Elyse as the lady was helped from the car by Armand. This woman, her son, and the beauty of Provence had become part of Angelina now. She wasn't likely to forget any of it, even if she didn't see them again.

Sarah and Raphaël were waiting for them beneath

the canopy of an elaborate entry where a man wearing a tuxedo opened the door with a bow. They had been expected. A woman wearing an expensive-looking black dress led them to a reserved table on the terrace. Low-hanging, tulip-shaped lamps offered a soft ambiance, and each table glowed with fine crystal and polished cutlery.

Beyond the covered terrace were the amethyst shades of a dying sunset. Palm trees thrust their stark fronds into the purple sky just outside the seating area adding a sense of otherworldliness to the scene. Angelina caught her breath at the beauty of it all. Who cared about the *food* served here? It was enough just to feast her eyes on the *view*.

A chair was pulled out for her by another attendant, and she sank into it with murmured thanks, hardly noticing the people around her. Slowly, however, she became aware there were other patrons in the space, all enjoying the warm summer night, the atmosphere of serenity, and the sound of waves breaking on the shore.

"*Le menu, madame,*" said a voice above her head and, as if in a dream, an ornately decorated card was placed into her hand. She glanced at it and realized it was all written in French. She knew her limitations and sought the advice of Armand who sat across from her, next to Elyse.

"Will you order for me please," she asked him with a sheepish grin. "My French does not extend this far."

"Me too please," Sarah piped up from beside her. As the man nodded with a polite inclination of his head, Angelina turned to her cousin with apology.

"I'm so sorry Sarah. I didn't even notice you sit down. It's lovely here, isn't it?"

"It's awesome," Sarah said. "I don't feel as though I should be allowed inside. I'm going to spill soup down my front or trip a waiter, I just know it."

Angelina stifled a giggle. She'd been thinking much the same thing and made a mental note to carefully calculate each move lest she stand up and take the tablecloth and its contents with her, or some such nonsense. It would be just like her, lately.

A small, fluted glass containing a deep red liquid arrived at each place setting. Everyone held their drinks aloft to clink and wish one another, "*Santé*." She took a sip of the sweet, effervescent liquid. It was delicious.

"Loosely translated, the word means *'To your health.'*" Angelina explained in a hushed undertone as Sarah poked her in the ribs to ask what the toast had meant. "I wonder what we're drinking?"

Overhearing them, Raphaël supplied more information. He held up the remainder of his glass to the light, tipping it back and forth. "Kir is a mixture of crème de cassis and either white wine or, in this case, champagne." When Sarah raised her eyebrows, he continued. "Crème de cassis is a liquor made from black currants. While a common apéritif in the whole of France, it is not so popular in Provence. People 'ere prefer pastis."

"And what is that?" Sarah snuggled close to him and gazed adoringly into his face.

He smiled down at her for a moment before answering. "Pastis is also an apéritif, but it is a powerful spirit that must be watered down a little before imbibing. It is flavoured with anise." Seeing Sarah's puzzled expression, he shrugged and looked to Angelina for help. "I don't know 'ow to explain the taste."

"Anise is an aromatic seed. Its flavour is similar to black licorice." Angelina took another drink from the delicate glass. "Correct?" She deferred the final word to Armand.

He nodded. "*Oui*."

Their first course arrived shortly thereafter, and well before Julien. A small white plate was set in front of Angelina, and she leaned forward to inhale the delicious scent as Armand translated what the server had said to her.

"Provençal stuffed squid," he announced. "Very fresh and stuffed with 'erbs, chard, and breadcrumbs, drizzled with anchovy vinaigrette." He cut a morsel and transported it to his mouth with a sigh of contentment. "*Délicieux*."

From the corner of her eye, Angelina could see Sarah take an exploratory poke at the dish. "It's not going to bite back, if that's what you're worried about," she whispered behind a lifted napkin. "It's *haute cuisine*. Just eat it."

A movement from across the room caught Angelina's attention. It was Julien. Her fork paused in its upward swing to watch him stride purposely down the aisle and slide into the empty chair next to his mother. Other women had noticed him too and she made herself focus on her tasty appetizer. It didn't matter to *her* who else found the man attractive.

Julien acknowledged each of them in turn with a few light words about the food, the environment, and the gorgeous vista they all would enjoy tonight. Except when it came to her, he had nothing to say. His grey, unfathomable eyes merely held her own for long seconds before he nodded briskly and set to work on his meal.

The evening passed too quickly for Angelina who was intent on savouring not only every new taste sensation, but every moment spent in this idyllic place.

A warm assortment of breads arrived, paired with both a rich yellow butter and one mixed with fresh herbs. Then they were served the main dish, the chef's own version of *confit de canard*. Armand explained that the duck would have been marinated for more than a day with salt, garlic, and thyme before being slow roasted in its own fat. It was served with roasted potatoes, carrots, and garlic on the side. Then came a cheese course with a tempting, melt-in-your-mouth selection of both hard and soft varieties.

Finally, as Angelina drew a deep breath and wished her dress was not quite so clingy, several choices of dessert were offered: chocolate soufflé, tarte Tatin made with a sweet, dark syrup, flakey pastry and apples, or a light lemon sorbet.

As well, with every new dish, the previous fragile glass of wine was whisked away and a new, more complimentary wine was poured.

When, at last, they were replete, a digestive was set before each person.

Angelina looked inquiringly at Armand who sat across from her, but it was Julien who answered. "It is called, liqueur de Farigoule, a traditional finale to an excellent meal 'ere in Provence. It is made from wild thyme, other 'erbs, and sugar."

She smiled her thanks, but Julien reached for his glass, avoiding her glance.

At last, it was time to leave. Armand stood first and excused himself.

"He wants to see 'is friend Marguerite," Elyse said, folding her cloth napkin and laying it on the table in front of her. "The chef was too busy with the dinner service to speak when we arrived and during the meal. It was very good, yes?"

"Yes." Angelina and Sarah answered in unison, and with enthusiasm. Dinner had defied all expectations.

"The food was marvelous," Angelina said. "I couldn't imagine a finer end to our visit. Thank you so much Elyse."

The woman inclined her head graciously, but nodded ever-so-slightly toward Julien. "It is not I who is paying for our evening," she said meaningfully.

"Julien," Angelina said with a loud, sharp edge to her voice. He swivelled toward her, leaving his contemplation of the outside scene to frown in answer to his name.

"*Oui?*"

"I mean, Julien," she cleared her throat and lowered her voice. "I understand it is you who has taken us out tonight. I would like to thank you. It was such a special evening."

He remained unsmiling. His eyes slid calmly down to pause on her mouth before rising up again.

Heat rose into her face, but she held his gaze.

"Yes, thank you," Sarah chimed in, breaking the spell.

Julien turned to her cousin and gave the girl a curt

nod. "You are most welcome, Sarah. I 'ope you 'ave enjoyed your stay with us?"

"Oh, I have," she gushed, clutching Raphaël's arm and raising her face for a kiss. "It's been wonderful."

Angelina averted her gaze. The display of affection between the two young people was almost sickening. Excusing herself, she made her way to the ladies' room where she leaned her clammy hands on the cool marble of the counter and stared into her brilliant green eyes.

The evening was over. All that was left was to drive home and get a good sleep. She straightened and, after refreshing her lipstick, she smoothed the glittering sequins of her dress, threw back her shoulders, and went out to find Elyse.

"I am so sorry *ma chère*," the lady hurried across the room to clasp her hands. "I cannot offer you a ride 'ome to the chateau. The friend of Armand's, Chef Marguerite, 'as asked 'im to join 'er after the restaurant is closed. It will be late and..." She shrugged.

Laughing, Angelina squeezed the lady's hands. "But that's fine. I'm happy to see you are enjoying yourself. I'm sure Sarah and Raphaël won't mind giving me a lift."

Elyse shook her head. "They 'ave left already I am afraid. I think they wish to be alone. You understand?" Elyse looked concerned, but her face relaxed as Angelina shook her head. "You don't mind then, if Julien takes you 'ome—do you?"

Actually, Angelina did mind, but she couldn't very well say that. "Of course not." She forced herself to look pleased. "Thank you again for a wonderful evening, Elyse. I'll see you in the morning over coffee." With another grateful squeeze, Elyse dropped Angelina's hands and scurried through a set of swinging doors to join Armand.

Angelina was glad Elyse was relaxing. The lady had been through so much of late. She spied the doors they had entered the restaurant through and made for them, expecting that Julien would be waiting in his car. But as her eyes adjusted to the gloom outside the restaurant, she saw him standing off to one side, staring out toward the sea.

"I thought we could take a short walk before retiring," he said quietly. "It is early after all."

"Of course," she replied, with all the politeness of a flight attendant. They fell into step with one another as they rounded the building, keeping to the shadows and on the sand.

"Most of the beaches on the Côte d'Azur are rocky," he said after a few moments. "This one is quite lovely, although I don't think it will be easy in those shoes." In the twilight she saw him look doubtfully at her feet. With a nervous laugh, she stopped and teetered on one foot, struggling to undo the straps.

"Allow me to 'elp you," Julien said. Taking her arm, he helped her to perch on a huge rock that protruded from the sand.

"Thanks." Angelina didn't trust herself to say more. His fingers were infinitely gentle as they slid open each clasp and slipped the shoes from her feet. Then, with the sandals dangling from his hand, he offered her his free one and pulled her upright. For a moment, they stood close. So close she felt the rough cloth of his jacket against her bare arms. Her breath caught and her mind raced, but he stepped back and gestured that she precede him along the beach.

"It was a lovely supper," she babbled. *Blast! That was the second time she'd talked about it.* She struggled to think of some sparkling conversation starter, but her mind was blank.

"Supper? That is a Canadian term I think," he said. His voice sounded vaguely amused. He hadn't teased her in days. She'd missed it.

"I suppose it is," she answered. "My family always refers to the evening meal as supper."

"And do you miss them? Your family?"

"No," she said breathlessly. Julien had caught her hand and swung it to and fro between them. "I mean... yes, at times I think of them, but I love it here." Her heart was starting the familiar wild beat that marked Julien's presence.

"I see. And your parents, are they retired? Wealthy?"

That was a puzzling question. Why would he possibly care if they were or weren't? "They are retired, yes and are—comfortable I would say. They sold the farm due to my father's ill health and now live in town, near my apartment. Why do you ask?"

"No reason." Julien entwined his fingers with hers. He sounded deliberately nonchalant. In the moments that followed, Angelina could tell he was struggling with another question, but she wasn't prepared for what he asked next.

"You 'ave no one special awaiting you at 'ome? A man you 'ave forgotten about while you are 'ere perhaps?"

Now that was downright rude. She wrenched her hand

from his grasp and shook it as though to rid herself of the tasteless inquiry.

"I think I told you before I am single. My boyfriend left me without a word some time ago. What possible business is that of yours?" Angelina folded her arms across her stomach and hugged herself. These were the last memories she wanted to be delving into.

"*Je suis désolé*," he hastened to add. "I did not mean any 'arm. It—it is something that 'as been on my mind lately. That is all."

"Because of your father and girlfriend?" Angelina blurted it out before thinking how he might respond to such a forthright question. Well, it served him right. He seemed to think he could ask her personal questions...so here was a taste of his own medicine.

"I suppose I deserved that," Julien said. They walked in silence and Angelina's anger faded. He had been through a lot the last several months. It had to have taken a toll on him.

"It 'as been difficult to accept the fact that Adrianne betrayed me. But knowing the man she cheated with was my father 'as been devastating, to say the least. I did not want my mother to suffer with this knowledge, so I kept it from 'er. As far as she knew, my father died alone in the car crash." He caught her hand again as they walked. "Please forgive me?" he asked.

"I can't imagine the pain you must have felt when you learned the truth," Angelina said at length. "I forgive you."

His thumb began to etch a mesmerizing circle on the palm of her hand. She closed her eyes, succumbing to the feelings it generated.

He didn't answer. Instead, Julien stopped and drew her around to face him. With his back to the sighing waves of the Mediterranean and the silvery glow of the moon, only *he* would be able to read her expression. His face was shrouded in darkness.

"You are a captivating woman on so many levels," he whispered. He reached out one hand and caressed her hair, pulling it forward and letting it slip through his fingers. "Your hair flows across your shoulders like ebony silk, *ma chère*."

Angelina swayed. His touch and the husky tone of his voice were playing tricks with her heart. She licked her lips and her face moved unconsciously toward his hand.

Julien groaned. His head dipped and his face came close to hers. His hands stole around her waist, drawing her against his unyielding chest. His thumbs continued their hypnotic circles as they now explored the small of her back.

She felt his breath in her hair before his lips blazed a trail of kisses across her cheek. And then, before the merest pause, he claimed her mouth with his.

The sweetness of his kiss unravelled her doubts. She reached for him, tangling her hands in his hair, wrapping her arms around his neck, and pulling him closer. Julien deepened the kiss. One hand remained firm on her back as the other gently cupped her chin, stroking the velvety softness of her face.

Then, with a ragged moan, he wrenched himself away. Angelina almost fell with his sudden departure. Steadying herself, she put both hands on her hips to draw several uneven breaths. She bent to pick up her clutch purse from where it had toppled into the sand and brushed the hair away from her face.

Julien stood looking out to sea, his hands shoved into his pockets. "Why do

I think you would be any different?" he muttered.

Turning, he walked toward her holding out her shoes. "I 'ad no right to do that. Please, let us go back to the car and I will drive you to the chateau. You 'ave no further fear of my advances."

She took the shoes and twisted the straps in her hands, trying to sort out what had just happened. She knew her feelings for this man went far deeper than she had allowed herself to believe. She was in love with him. However, accepting the fact brought her tortured heart no relief. He had spurned her yet again and she didn't know why. *Hadn't they dealt with his doubts?* It wasn't likely she'd ever know what was wrong now, as she was going home tomorrow.

They sped back through the night Julien keeping a tight-lipped silence the entire way. Tentatively, thinking to open the channels of discussion, Angelina had asked him if he had been able to hire anyone to fill the driver's position, but he had responded with a brusque "Non" and that had been the end of their conversation.

When the tires of the Lexus ground to a halt outside the chateau, Angelina did not wait for his assistance. Wrenching the door open, she scrambled outside and slammed the door behind her wishing she had never come to this wretched place, knowing in her heart of hearts that all she wanted to do was stay.

CHAPTER 15

The next morning, Angelina rolled over in bed and held a hand to her throbbing brow. She didn't usually get headaches, but the events of the previous evening, coupled with several glasses of wine, had done her no favours. She groaned as she glanced at her watch and a realization of the time smote her squarely between the eyes. It was a quarter past ten. Why had no one woken her? She didn't want to lounge in bed for her last few hours in Provence.

Hurriedly she peeled back the thick coverlet and rolled free, clutching a hand to her forehead as her feet thumped onto the floor. First, she needed a painkiller from her purse, and then a shower.

The sun had already begun its steady climb into the sky before she was dressed in jeans and a t-shirt that had seen better days. It was too much effort to look good when dealing with a headache, and she wanted to be comfortable when she navigated Paris with Sarah and her huge amounts of luggage. Pulling her hair into a ponytail, Angelina walked gingerly to the winding staircase and listened for signs of life.

There were none. In fact, as she walked into the kitchen to make herself a coffee, she found it completely empty. Thankfully, she'd watched Armand enough times to know how to run the elaborate machine he used for making cappuccinos, lattes, and the café crème she was so fond of.

Throwing herself down on a chair at the table she sipped the fragrant brew. It just wouldn't be the same back home. Her old drip machine chugged out a decent cup of java, but it wasn't nearly as tasty as this. She sighed, put her feet up on the chair across from her, and wondered where everyone was.

Doubtless, Sarah was spending every last moment with Raphaël. That was understandable. And Julien would certainly not hang around the chateau when there was a chance he might run into her. *The horror.* Yes, she was feeling bitter and didn't care.

Elyse suddenly rounded the corner. She stopped short and stared at Angelina with red-rimmed eyes.

"What is it?" Angelina scrambled to her feet, fear striking her heart, and ran to the woman's side. "Something's happened. Are you alright?" Elyse sagged and Angelina half caught the lady in her arms and helped her to a chair.

Elyse collapsed onto the table, weeping hysterically. Angelina didn't know what to do. Should she run to find someone? Julien perhaps? Or Raphaël? They might know what was wrong. Instead, she knelt on the tiles beside Elyse's chair and wrapped her arms around the woman's shaking shoulders.

For a time, the only sounds to be heard were rasping sobs. Then Elyse calmed a little and began to take deep, choking breaths. Wordlessly, she lifted her tousled head and laid a sodden piece of paper on the table.

"You want me to read it?" Angelina straightened and pulled a chair close to Elyse. She picked up the official looking paper and scanned it. The ink was blurred in spots. Plus, it was all in French.

"I'm sorry, Elyse. I can't read much French, but it looks like it was sent to your husband from an office in Paris."

With a huge sigh, Elyse sat up and motioned toward the counter. "*S'il te plait.*" Following her gaze, Angelina noticed tissues and hurried to grab the box. Upon her return, Elyse pulled several into her hands, mopped her eyes, and blew her nose.

Haltingly, she began. "This letter is the one you found in the jacket from your room." She took a breath. "Georges was wearing that coat when 'e was killed, and the letter must 'ave been in the pocket. I 'adn't looked at it until this morning. To be honest, I was afraid it might contain divorce papers." She stopped and looked out the window for a long moment.

"When I overheard Natalie telling you that Georges had run away with Adrianne, I was devastated. I didn't know what 'ad gone wrong between my 'usband and I, but I never thought 'e would 'ave an affair. Yet, once the idea entered my head, I started believing it." She turned to Angelina with brimming eyes. "And now, thanks to this letter, I know 'e was *not* 'aving an affair." Elyse snatched the paper up and waved it before covering her mouth with a hand to catch another sob.

Angelina sat in stunned silence.

Pulling herself together, Elyse clasped the letter to her chest. "This letter is from Adrianne's uncle, an oncologist in Paris that is very 'ard to get an appointment with. Thanks to Adrianne, the doctor had agreed to meet with my dear Georges privately, after hours to determine what could be done to 'elp. She was taking 'im there, the day they died."

Angelina reached out to rub Elyse's shoulder as the woman's frail frame began to heave with emotion.

"I did not know my dear Georges 'ad been diagnosed with cancer." She held the paper out and scanned its contents once more. "It says their office received the records that were sent from our family doctor, and gives a date and time for Georges to be at the appointment. It was the same day they were in the accident." She blotted her eyes again.

"That must 'ave been why he grew silent and pulled away. He was dealing with the burden of this terrible illness alone. Georges always tried to protect me from the world outside these walls." She squeezed her eyes shut. "*Mon cher mari* was not leaving me, 'e was doing 'is best to spare me the fear and worry 'e knew I would feel." Her eyes pleaded with Angelina to understand. "He was wrong, of course. I would 'ave wanted to know and to support 'im, but...that was the choice 'e made." She took another shuddering breath.

"I don't know why Georges chose to confide in Julien's girlfriend. Maybe she mentioned 'er famous uncle, the doctor, and Georges asked her about 'im." She smiled tremulously at Angelina's shocked expression. "Yes, I knew my son was dating his manager. But I also knew he did not wish it to be known. He and Adrianne were never right for one another. A mother has a sense of these things." She patted her heart.

Gently, Elyse kissed the letter. "Maybe, if Georges would 'ave told me, things would 'ave ended differently, but we will never know. I must console myself with knowing that he loved me until the end."

Angelina's mind was reeling. Elyse was free of the torment that had held her captive. She knew what had caused her husband to withdraw and best of all, knew he hadn't been running away with Julien's girlfriend.

"Julien needs to know," she stuttered. "All this time —he was trying to spare you too!" She realized how freeing this news was for the whole family. "Sarah and I have to leave soon, but perhaps I can find your sons and bring them to hear the truth from you?"

Angelina stood up and then sat down, her agitation mounting.

"Yes, my dear, I think that would be a very good idea." Her eyes narrowed. "You care for my son, yes?" It was a sudden question and took Angelina unawares.

"Yes." She blurted it out before she had time to think, then clapped a hand over her mouth. She should not have told his mother any such thing. She should just melt into the distance and forget about these people and this place.

"I thought so," Elyse smiled through her tears. "Julien has what you would call, a hard head. He has been married to this estate since 'e was only a teenager, but women 'ave always thrown themselves at 'im. He dated a few, but they were only interested in 'is money, of course, not in the man 'e is." She twisted the tissues in her hands and leaned back in her chair with a sigh.

"It changed 'im. He trusted no one until 'e started dating Adrienne and then, she was found dead in a car with 'is father on their way to visit the city of love. I can see what it looked like to 'im, because it looked the same way to me once I knew of it. It would alter a man's thinking." She paused. "I believe 'e cares for you too."

Angelina's could feel her face flushing. "He's barely ever around me. How do you know he cares?"

Without answering, Elyse folded the letter and slid it into the pocket of one of her trademark long, colourful dresses, rolled her tissues into a ball, and stood to deposit them in the waste bin. Then she turned slowly and regarded Angelina.

"I know for that exact reason. Because 'e is never around. He stays away, because 'e is afraid to 'ave feelings of love. Afraid to trust someone again. Relationships 'ave never been good for 'im." She fingered the letter in her pocket and moved toward the door. "Until you came along, I would 'ave agreed with 'im. Now, go see if you can find my sons and I will call my daughter. There is not much time before you must leave for the airport"

❧

ANGELINA HAD READ ABOUT LE MISTRAL, THE WIND of Provence. It was a violent, northwesterly wind that grew in velocity and power as it funneled through the Rhône and Durance River valleys and passed on to meet the Mediterranean Sea. But she hadn't experienced it until today. Zipping up her light jacket, she leaned into the gale as she ran down the steps of the chateau with the keys to the Citroën in her hand.

She'd seen evidence of the wind in the Provencal landscape. Many of the trees were permanently bent toward the south, and rooftops were littered with bricks and heavy stones to keep the tiles from blowing away. They told a tale of the wind better than words could. Now she fought with the tiny car door as she yanked it open and then wrenched it shut before the wind tore it off.

She turned the key, revved the motor, and considered which way to go first. The store would be a start. Driving against the wind was one thing, but running against it was quite another, yet she made it to the door and pulled it shut behind her.

"Have you seen either of the Belliveau men?" she asked the teenager behind the till, bending over to catch her breath.

"No madame, not for some time. Monsieur Julien went to Marseille on business this morning. We don't expect him to return until late afternoon." The boy shifted from foot to foot. "And your cousin and Monsieur Raphaël left about an hour ago, in one of the trucks used for hauling grapes. He said he was going to show her the view from the highest point of the property."

"I see. Thank you." Angelina swung around and marched back out. *So, Julien wasn't even planning on being around to say goodbye. Nice. Was that really a guy that cared? Nope.*

She glanced at her watch as she hurried to the little

car and wheeled it around to begin the trek up the rocky mountainside. At least she would find *one* of the brothers. Plus, there was only two hours until she and Sarah were due to check in at the airport. What was the girl thinking?

As she bumped along the rocky path, Angelina was aware that the little car, with its low clearance, wouldn't make it very far up the mountainous terrain. Soon she would be forced to walk. The mistral buffeted the little car and debris smacked against the driver's door causing her to jump. Until on a rocky ledge, she thought she felt the tiny car tip from the force of the elements outside. It could have been her imagination, but she wasn't taking any chances. The path was nearly non-existent now anyway. It was time to stop.

Pulling the Citroën off the road into an area just large enough to wedge it, she battled to open the door against the wind. The gusts were worse at the higher elevation. They whistled around the chalky cliffs and howled through gullies eroded by time. Angelina shoved the keys in her pocket and began to climb. The road had all but disappeared and she followed little more than a faint set of fresh tracks.

Having gone for many a walk during her time at the chateau, she had an idea where Raphaël might take Sarah and she slogged on with her head down, leaning against the onslaught of wind. As she rounded a cliff and looked up, she saw the truck, half of its back end hanging over a cliff that dropped at least 200 metres to the garrigue below, with one wheel rotating uselessly in the air.

Fear clutched at her heart as she broke into a run,

dodging boulders and leaping over rocks in her haste to get there and somehow help. Panting, she pulled herself over a ledge that made her wonder what Raphaël had been thinking to drive this high, and onto the highest peak.

Raphaël was revving the motor over and over causing dust and exhaust to rise like clouds of dense smoke before it was torn away in the gale. The motor screamed, forcing the rear wheels to rotate. He hung out the driver's door, watching, frantically trying to get the truck back onto solid ground. But it was hopeless.

Angelina ran closer and assessed the situation. The back dual wheels on the passenger side were still on solid ground, but the constant spinning had ground them deep into the limestone. They now sat in a smooth hollow. The other side of the vehicle hung in midair, and the truck tilted precariously. Sarah stood some distance away clasping and unclasping her arms while weeping hysterically.

Her cousin was fine, and Angelina paid her no further notice. This truck, and Raphaël needed her. She ran around to the young man and hollered at him, hoping her words wouldn't be whipped away and lost in the wild wind.

"Take it out of gear, apply the brake and hold the wheel steady. I'm going to give the back wheels some traction." He nodded; his white face pinched with fear.

Darting to and fro she gathered branches from long-dead trees, craggy rocks the size of her fist and anything else she could see that might work to offer the wheels something to grab onto. She pulled her t-shirt free of her jeans and used it as a means to carry what she found to the truck. Then she threw everything into the pit the back wheels had dug. Her final move was to wedge a larger rock *behind* the wheels, so that with any luck at all, the truck would not roll backward any farther than it had. It was in danger of going over the cliff and taking Raphaël with it.

She shouted at Sarah and motioned that the girl come help. She was clearly beside herself with fear, but Angelina somehow got her cousin to stand on the running board of the passenger side as a counterweight. Then she rushed around again to Raphaël.

"When I say go, I want you to slide as far as you can to the opposite side of the cab and stay there," she yelled. "I'm hoping you and Sarah can stabilize the weight just enough that the back duals will grab, hold, and pull us out of here. Got it?"

"Oui!" he called. There was not a moment to lose. The truck rocked in the wind and lurched a little further to the side that had fallen off the cliff.

"GO!" Angelina yelled, lunging behind the wheel as Raphaël slid across to lean heavily against the other side. She slammed the clutch into the floorboards, shifted into the lowest gear she could, and released the brake. But rather than punching the accelerator, she let the forward momentum of the engine do all the work. The motor growled and bore down. Slowly and surely the back wheels slipped and then caught the debris Angelina had used for traction. Ever so slightly, the truck started to move forward.

Moments later they were on solid ground.

Angelina took the truck out of gear, applied the brake, and slumped over the wheel as Sarah ripped open the door and cheered. Raphaël sat with his head in his hands. After a moment he turned an ashen face to her.

"To say *merci beaucoup*, is not enough to express my gratitude," he said. "You are an angel sent in my hour of greatest need. I don't know 'ow you knew to do all that."

She lifted her head and found that her hands were shaking, but her voice was strong. "I'm glad I could help," she said simply.

Sarah climbed inside the cab and threw her arms around the young man. She looked at Angelina, and with pride in her voice she explained. "My cousin is a truck driver back home. You might not think so to look at her, but she's one of the best."

Raphaël's eyes widened. "*Tres bien!* No wonder you are so good," he said. "I 'ave not often driven such large trucks, but there was no other vehicle available today. I wanted to show Sarah the view. Backing up to turn around was a mistake. I went too far. Wait, what is the time?" he asked with sudden concern. "You 'ave to leave soon."

Angelina and Sarah looked at one another and then at their wrists. "We have an hour to get to the airport," Angelina groaned, throwing the truck into gear once more. I'll drive it down to the Citroën and you take the car to the chateau. Deal?" she asked Raphaël.

"Deal."

They rumbled down the craggy limestone mountain as fast as was safe to travel. When they saw the tiny yellow car appear around a bend, Angelina fished in her pocket and gave Raphaël the keys and the information she'd meant to share with him all along.

"Your mother has something to tell you. It's important you see her as soon as possible." She glanced at the way he and Sarah clung to one another in the passenger seat. "After you say your goodbyes of course." She grinned as the truck ground to a halt.

"Actually, I think I'll go with him if that's alright," Sarah asked, clutching Raphaël's hand.

Angelina only waved them out of the cab with a laugh and continued on her way down to park the truck behind the shop. She could ill-afford the time to run back to the chateau, but there wasn't any choice. So, she jogged up the path and through the garden to enter the house through the terrace door.

With no one around she was spared explanations and dashed up to her room to give it a final sweep with her eyes as she grabbed the old backpack and her brand-new case before rolling it out the door. Sarah met her in the hallway and together they hurried downstairs.

Elyse stood in the foyer with an arm around her youngest son and a smile on her face. Even at a glance, Angelina could tell that the woman was free of the fear and unhappiness that had plagued her. Now, that she was assured of Georges love, she could begin to properly grieve, and move on with her life.

Sarah walked outside, arm in arm with Raphaël after hugging Elyse and thanking her for the wonderful visit. Now Elyse held Angelina.

"Raphaël told me what you did," she whispered into Angelina's ear. "I cannot believe that you can drive such vehicles as that." She shook her head. "Thank you for all you did today, my dear, and for finding the letter. I am so glad to call you my friend. Please contact me when you are 'ome safe?"

"I will." Angelina couldn't trust herself to say more. Her throat felt as dry as the limestone hills behind the chateau. She blinked rapidly.

"Julien meant to be back in order to see you off," his mother went on. "I am not sure why 'e is not, but I know 'e will be sorry to miss saying *au revoir*. Come back one day, yes?" Elyse lifted her hands to hold Angelina's face and kiss each cheek.

"Yes," Angelina said dutifully, but not truthfully. She would never be back. The idyllic, golden summer was over, and her heart felt as though it might break in two.

They piled into the tiny yellow Citroën. With tearful waves to Elyse, who stood in the chateau doorway, Raphaël started the engine, and they motored down the long driveway. Angelina was in the back seat again, trying vainly to swallow the lump in her throat. The tiny car pulled onto the main road as she held a hand to her forehead. It had been a difficult and emotional day. She wouldn't allow herself to think of Julien and studiously stared down the road ahead, refusing to cry.

And then, suddenly, there he was, waving for them to stop as he spun towards them in his powerful car.

Raphaël had already seen him and was pulling into an approach. Julien followed and his door was flung wide as he hurriedly jumped out and strode toward them.

Angelina's hands were instantly clammy. She wanted to leap from the car and run into his arms, but worried she should stay aloof, sitting in the car as though she couldn't possibly care less.

She gulped and reached for the door. Sarah had already flung herself outside and was hugging him. Angelina unfolded herself from the tiny back seat, rose to her feet and shoved her hands down her jeans. She thought what a mess she must look like after the trouble they'd just had.

Adjusting the tie in her hair, she tried to smooth the flyaway strands that blew fiercely around her face. She met Julien's eyes over Sarah's shoulder. It was as though they burned into her very soul.

Sarah stepped away and looked at her cousin expectantly. Angelina didn't care what her actions looked like anymore. She covered the space between herself and Julien in seconds. And, just like she'd noticed the night before, when they touched it felt as though the world had slipped away leaving the two of them at its core.

Wrapping her in his arms, he leaned down to bury his face in the dark hair that whirled around her. When he leaned his face against hers, she thought he might have groaned, but the wind stole any sounds away. He pulled back, his grey eyes piercing her own. She fancied they looked hungrily at her, dropping to linger for long seconds on her lips. At length, he spoke like an automaton—stiff and robotic. Yet she had the distinct feeling it was not what he had wanted to say. Or maybe that was her hopeful imagination.

"I am so glad you accompanied your cousin on this visit. Sorry I was away. I 'ad every intention of returning early to wish you a safe journey, but I was detained in Marseille." His hands grasped her upper arms and his thumbs, she was sure unconsciously, began the same, rhythmic motion they had the night before. Her knees wobbled. If he kissed her now, she knew she would blurt out her true feelings and take her chances on being turned away.

But he didn't. Instead, he stepped back, and his hands fell to his sides. "I wish you all 'appiness Angelina. I 'ave enjoyed our time together and I wish you a *bon voyage*."

"Thank you," she croaked. Clearing her throat she tried again, louder. "And I want to thank you and your family for making us feel so welcome. I truly love Provence and..." she had almost said, *him*, but caught herself in time. "And I appreciated getting to know your mother. She is a sweet, wonderful woman."

Julien backed toward his car. "I must allow you to leave. You will miss your plane reservation. It departs soon, *n'est-ce pas?*" He shouted into the gale-force wind that tugged at his suit jacket and wound its fingers through his hair.

"Yes," Angelina said. She felt the chill of the mistral bite into her clothes. Her hand almost lifted in beckoning. She had a strong urge to call to him; to beg him to come back, so she could explain how she felt. She cared nothing for the onlookers. Emotions had grown, expanding in her heart until it felt as though they might burst.

But she could see his mind was made up. She did not fit into his lifestyle of opulence and excess. She was a humble country girl who drove trucks and loved the simple things in life. It could never have worked and now was not the time to try.

With that, Julien turned, levered himself back behind the wheel of his car and waited for them to pull away. Angelina and Sarah climbed back inside the Citroën and snapped on their seatbelts. Raphaël gunned the motor of their little yellow car and peeled off down the road leaving Julien in the ever-widening gap between his world and Angelina's.

Fortunately, the queue wasn't too long, and the two women raced to make the last boarding call. They had almost missed the flight altogether, but stopping to speak to Julien had been worth it. Angelina sank into her window seat, closed her eyes, and recalled the final moments before distance parted her from Julien forever. She had slid across the back seat to stare out the window shamelessly. Her last sight of him was of his eyes riveted on hers. He lifted three fingers to his lips and blew them to her in a final gesture of farewell.

And then they were gone.

CHAPTER 16

Angelina's body physically ached with the thought that she would never see Julien again. A vision of his laughing face, taunting her on the plane at their first meeting, floated in her mind. Then, the kiss blown to her through the window at their final goodbye. That had touched her heart. It felt almost hard to breathe from the pain of it all.

She stared out the aircraft window as the last few glimpses of Provence sped away beneath her. Rows upon rows of olive trees marched along the sun-baked earth and into the white chalky hills while toy cars coiled their way along the narrow winding roads between them. Soon, the plane was too high to see anything more than the clouds below. She rested her head back on the seat, using her fingers to stem the tide of tears that threatened to overwhelm her. Could she ever forget the man?

She thought of last night and her eyes fluttered shut in remembrance. She could still feel Julien's arms around her and the taste of his lips on hers as the sea air had caressed their bodies. It was heavenly. Why had he brought it to such an abrupt halt? It must have been a lack of trust brought on by Adrianne's supposed betrayal, and the money-hungry females of the neighbourhood? That's what his mother seemed to think.

Julien had also asked her about her family and whether they were wealthy. She'd thought it was a strange question at the time, but in light of what Elyse had told her—perhaps it all made sense. He was accustomed to disingenuous people. Yet, she hadn't been the one that initiated the intimate moments they'd shared —he had.

He was wrong about her too. She didn't care a flying fig about money, which was the truth, but she *was* penniless. And, if he ever found out what she actually did for a living—she was almost positive he wouldn't be interested in her at all. If the beautiful Natalie was anything to go by, as far as the sort of woman he might find appealing, there was no way he'd want a truck driver for a girlfriend. She almost laughed at the thought, but it caught in her throat on a sob.

She reached for the hotel reservations tucked into her purse and consulted the address again. She'd planned on booking a hotel in the heart of Paris for one last splurge with Sarah. Thankfully, she'd realized in time that her cousin's three heavy suitcases, and her own bag containing the olive oil and wine, plus the old backpack she'd slung over one shoulder, were too much to lug all over Paris. Instead, she booked the two of them into an airport hotel.

Once they'd arrived, left their luggage in the room,

and changed into light dresses and sandals, they took the train into the City of Lights.

Although Sarah had shed a few tears as they left Raphaël in the airport terminal, she had recovered her bubbly good spirits quickly. The short flight to the Charles de Gaulle Airport near Paris, was filled with Sarah's endless reflections on her holiday with a distinct emphasis on Raphaël. She chattered about every detail of the fabulous things she'd seen and done with him and how they were making plans for him to visit her in Canada soon. While Angelina was happy for her cousin, it was a little tough to stomach.

Her own heart felt like it had shattered into a million pieces. Nonetheless, she maintained a brave face for her cousin.

Angelina shifted her cross-body purse into a more comfortable position as she sat across from her cousin on the underground train. She'd read up on the best vantage point to see the Eiffel Tower for the first time, and she meant to make this a memorable visit for Sarah even if her heart wasn't in it.

Some time later, they emerged from the Metro, climbed up the steps to street level, and to the famous Trocadero Square. Angelina grew excited to see the marvelous monument despite the gnawing ache in her chest. Soon they gazed across the Seine River to the Eiffel Tower. It was magnificent.

All the obligatory photos were taken, and then began the long walk down the hill and cross the Seine on *Pont d'Iena*, the bridge that spanned the river at this point.

They had the rest of the day to explore Paris. What

better place to start than *La Tour Eiffel?* It should have been thrilling for her, but she couldn't drum up any enthusiasm. Perhaps, once she was home with her family and life got back to normal, she'd feel better.

Reaching the opposite bank of the river, they looked up at the massive structure before crossing the street to be even closer. Angelina remembered it had been built to be one of the main attractions at the Paris World's Fair in 1889. What a remarkable achievement for the people who were part of its creation.

Throngs of people bustled to and fro on the sidewalks nearby. Tour buses purred slowly up the street and discharged further numbers to add to the madness.

"I need a drink," said Sarah. She'd spied a small, covered building that offered everything from ice cream to Champagne. Already walking away, she called over her shoulder, "Want something?"

"No. I'll wait here for you," Angelina waved her away. "Just don't get swept away in the crowds and carried off to see Napoleon's tomb without me." She attempted a grin, then when Sarah disappeared into the maze of people, she turned back to the tower.

A taxi pulled between two buses across the street, and a man climbed out to pay the driver. He looked remarkably like someone she knew.

Julien?

It couldn't possibly be him. Surely she was seeing things. Angelina looked away, but only for a second. When she glanced back the man dodged traffic as he jogged across the street against the light. Cars honked. He lifted his head and caught her eye.

It was him.

"Salut," he said, coming to a stop in front of her as though it were commonplace for them to run into one another in front of the Eiffel Tower. He looked flustered and serious.

She felt as though she'd been turned to stone. Was something wrong? Was Elyse alright? How in the world had he found them? And why? They stared at one another for a long moment.

"What are you doing here?" she finally managed. "How did you know…"

"Where else would you go on your first trip to Paris?" He shrugged. "Actually, I went first to the Arc de Triomphe. It was pure luck that I found you so quickly." His face looked almost as grey as his eyes. He ran both hands through his hair and grumbled with annoyance as someone bumped him.

"Is something wrong with Elyse?"

"No. She is fine. I need to talk with you—privately," he said with urgency. "Where is Sarah?"

Angelina was still too shocked by his appearance to answer. Her mouth opened and then closed. This couldn't be happening.

"She's over there waiting in a line for a drink," she said, waving a hand toward her cousin. "I want to know why you're here?"

Julien had never looked so rumpled. He was wearing the same clothes she'd seen him in last and his hair stood almost perpendicular to his head.

"I 'ave to tell you…I am sorry for misjudging you," he said in a rush. "*Ma mere* told me that you saved my brother today." His voice broke. "Apparently, she knew all along what you did to earn your way in this world, because Sarah 'ad told 'er. But I didn't know."

"What possible difference does that make?" Angelina was confused. Had the man rushed across the country to tell her he approved of her career? Nothing he was saying made sense.

"It means, you are poor, but it is not something you concern yourself with or are trying to leave behind. You are 'appy with your choices in life, *n'est-ce pas?* You do whatever it takes to earn a living by using your considerable talent. I admire your determination and tenacity... and am astounded at your ability."

"Fabulous," she said dryly.

Was this man patronizing her now? What was wrong with him?

"So, let me get this straight. You caught the very next flight out of Marseille and scoured the streets of Paris, just to tell me that you, Julien Belliveau, endorse my life choices, and my poverty? Why didn't you text, or write an email to announce this amazing fact?" She drew a breath. "Here's a news flash for you. I don't need your approval. Driving trucks is what I do and I'm good at it. I may live a simpler life than yours, but that doesn't make my existence any less worthwhile or something I strive to get away from. I'm happy in Canada and I don't need the help of any man to improve on it."

To her surprise, Julien began to laugh. "You're beautiful when you are in a temper." His face took on a mischievous look. "I didn't 'ave to wait for the next plane. I 'ave my own."

She felt even angrier. "Have you lost your mind?" she asked forcefully. Folding her arms across her chest, she took a step back. "You think I came here to win over the affluent Julien Belliveau, don't you? Because, by your standards I'm poor and therefore all I would want in life is to catch a wealthy man?" Anger caused her voice to rise, and people began to give them a wide berth. "Well, you can shove your stupid ideas where the sun don't shine," she yelled. "How's that for an interesting saying?"

Julien sobered at her words. "No. Angelina," he stepped forward and lifted his hands in a placating gesture. "I mean, yes, I suppose I did think you were just another one of those women who have appeared at the chateau, 'oping to become the next Madame Belliveau, but I was wrong. I know you are not one of them and I apologize for thinking it." His gaze shifted to stare at the lowering sun over her shoulder

"What you did today..." His voice trailed off into nothingness before he rallied. "Quite simply, I am in your debt, and I beg your forgiveness."

At that moment, someone fell against Angelina, hard. With a yelp, she tumbled into Julien, but before she fell, he opened his arms and caught her, bringing her close to his body. He held her there. Although she was still seething at his foolish assumptions, she relaxed against his broad chest for just a moment before trying to pull away.

But Julien would not relinquish his hold. "You fell into my arms when we first met. I believe it was fate, *mon amour*."

My love? He was calling her, his love. Angelina stood still, but her heart began to race. She gazed up at him.

"It is true. I love you, Angelina." His grey eyes held

hers, flashing like emeralds, and his hands spanned her waist to draw her even closer "I ask you to forgive my foolishness and come back to the estate as soon as possible, so we may continue to learn more of one another."

"You what?" Angelina felt like a deer caught in the headlights of a car. She hadn't registered anything he'd said past telling her he loved her. Her breathing was rapid.

He leaned in then. Amid the cheers of all the people waiting for the light to go green, he kissed her, the sensation of his lips moving against her own like a sweet balm.

Regardless of onlookers, Julien took time before lifting his head. When he did, he leaned back to look at her with infinite tenderness, Angelina raised wondering fingers to her mouth. Then, she placed a hand on either side of his face and kissed him back.

"I love you too," she said, smiling into his face. "I can't believe you came after me—and found me in the midst of thirteen million tourists." She grinned. "Of course, you could have just asked your mother for my cell phone number."

"I would 'ave torn the city apart to find you," he said, enfolding her once again in his arms and nuzzling her ear. "I did not think of that. I only thought to find you in person and tell you how I feel. Will you return to the chateau to stay with us as soon as you are able?"

"Wait a moment," she paused as a sudden chill struck her heart and she pushed him away. "Did you kiss Sarah that day in her room? After you'd just kissed me in the pool?"

His face took on a puzzled expression and then he smiled. "Your cousin is a delightful child, but that is all. I 'ave never kissed her and 'ad no intention of ever doing so. She wished to come to France, and I thought a distraction might 'elp my mother...to have visitors. Sarah had different ideas, but that is all they were. The romantic ideas of a young girl."

Angelina could feel the worry on her forehead melt away like snow in spring. "Okay, that makes sense."

"Now, back to your question, I'd love to come back here." She slid her arms around his waist and laid her head on his chest. Her heart sang with joy.

"Julien?" Sarah's disbelieving voice sliced into their rosy world.

They turned, Julien catching Angelina's hand and pulling it up to his lips.

Laughing, Angelina turned tear-filled eyes to her cousin. "He came to find me. Isn't that wonderful?"

Sarah nodded. Blankly she stared from one to the other of them until a slow grin stretched across her face.

"Does this mean we can double-date?"

EPILOGUE

The throaty roar of the truck's engine filled Angelina's ears as she reversed down a narrow path between endless rows of olive trees. She kept a close eye on her rear-view mirror, but glanced up for a moment to acknowledge a few of the seasonal workers that had arrived at the estate to work during this time. Then, backing onto a gravel track at the end of the field, she stopped, shifted gears, and set off for the mill.

Twilight was falling over the Provencal landscape. It was late in October, and this would be her last load for the season. Rumbling along, she gazed at the many groups of people concluding their labour and rolling up their long nets.

She smiled. Most had worked with long, lightweight rakes that combed through the branches of the trees, tugging the fruit from where it nestled among the leaves. Other people insisted on climbing the trees themselves, pulling the olives by hand and depositing

ONE GOLDEN SUMMER

them into aprons that hung over one shoulder with a large built-in pocket. Beneath the gnarly branches, nets had been laid in a wide ring to catch any fruit that fell.

Angelina revelled in the sight, grateful to be back in Provence and part of the harvest. She bumped onto the main road and sped up only a little before signalling to turn in at the familiar entrance to the estate. She cranked the wheel of the truck, guiding it toward the factory where the multi-coloured fruit would be dumped into a hopper and carried off to begin the extraction process.

Julien was somewhere inside the plant, overseeing operations and working alongside the trusted members of his staff. She would see him tonight, over a late dinner with Elyse. They planned to celebrate the end of a successful harvest. She contemplated the time between her return to Canada and now as she fuelled the truck.

It had been seven months since Georges Belliveau had died. Everyone who loved Elyse was thrilled to see she was enjoying her life once more. She visited friends, helped with the occasional tour group, and had held several successful parties at the chateau where everyone had miraculously behaved themselves.

After learning the real reason Georges had been driving to Paris, Julien was a new man. Angelina shook her head, marvelling at the burden he must have carried when he believed his father was having an affair with Adrianne, his fiancé. The truth had set Julien free.

Lia and her family were often over to visit. Angelina appreciated her growing friendship with Elyse's daughter and awaited the birth of Lia's second child along with the rest of the family. Her baby could arrive any day now. The Belliveau family had accepted Angelina with open arms.

Angelina frowned, her thoughts shifting over to a man who had begun to frequent the Belliveau Estate with annoying regularity. Edward Wright was an olive oil buyer from London, England, who had first visited the estate in hopes of purchasing a large quantity of the product wholesale, so that he could import it back to his own distributer in the UK. However, after meeting Elyse while she led a tour one afternoon, he had stayed in Marseille far longer than he had originally intended. The man had showed up to visit the family almost every night this week, but Elyse appeared to enjoy his company. So, Julien tolerated his presence with easygoing friendliness. Angelina suspected there was more going on in Edward's mind, than just the discussion of olives. However, she was pretty sure Elyse saw him as nothing more than a pleasant man who came rather often to talk to Julien. Besides, he'd need to return to the UK at some point.

Angelina wondered how Julien and his siblings would feel if their mother fell in love. At fifty-five, she was still a young woman. It was reasonable to expect she'd meet someone special again one day. Even though Georges had been the love of her life, and she'd vowed she would never be interested in any other man, one never knew what was around the corner. Only time would tell.

After parking the truck in the compound and

locking the gate, Angelina flipped her ponytail over her shoulder and began the walk up to the chateau. Taking a deep, contented breath, she gazed at her surroundings. The setting sun cast an amber glow on the world, bringing it into radiant focus. Vineyards blazed with the deep golden shades of autumn to the west and to the east, while the creamy white cliffs gleamed. In between them, the last rays of sunshine warmed the air with a dusky yellow luminosity. It was gorgeous and she was indescribably happy.

Quickening her pace, Angelina soon arrived at the front steps and took them two at a time. She wanted to have a shower and wear something pretty for Julien as well as in honour of the day and the special meal Armand was preparing. For several weeks now she'd been working on the estate wearing jeans and t-shirts. It was time to glam herself up a bit.

It hadn't taken long, once arriving back in Canada with Sarah, for Angelina to give notice at her apartment building, pack up her few things and store them at her parents while she waited for her work visa. Being able to prove she had gainful employment in France with working on the estate as a driver, meant there was less difficulty in obtaining the documents needed to return to Provence.

Angelina had even gone back to the gravel company to see a few of the men she had worked with. Kenton was back at university, which was great news, and Glenn watched sheepishly from the doorway of his office while she spoke with the guys and told them where she would be working next. They were amazed, but happy, warning her jokingly to beware of French men. She grinned in acknowledgement of their teasing, not telling them her heart had already been won.

Her parents and sister were the hardest ones to leave behind. She would miss them and they her, but she assured Marcie she would fly back for the birth of her nephew (Marcie had been thrilled to announce it would be a boy).

Everyone remarked on Angelina's evident joy and were pleased for her happiness. Her parents even promised to come for a visit if she stayed on in France.

Sarah had remained in touch with Raphaël for the first month after her return home, but distance definitely did not make her heart grow fonder. She soon met and fell madly in love with a carpet installer from Winnipeg, Manitoba, the city where she'd grown up. Although, ultimately, that didn't last long either, Angelina had high hopes for her young cousin. Sarah had recently exhibited signs of growing up when she'd enrolled at the local university to pursue a degree in education.

As soon as possible, Angelina had flown back to France and the Belliveau Estate to be with Julien. What followed was nothing short of idyllic.

He had taken her to visit ancient sites, wander through historic little villages, experience the energy and life of Marseille, and generally bask in the remaining weeks of summer. All this was accomplished hand in hand as they learned more about one another and fell more deeply in love. At least, she felt that way. Julien hadn't said much about his emotions since finding her in Paris.

She stepped into a dress she'd purchased from a shop while visiting a nearby village with Elyse. It was a pale mauve chiffon with sprigs of tiny fuchsia flowers dotting the material. She lifted her arms in the mirror to admire the pretty bell sleeves and short full skirt. Yes, this would do nicely.

She applied her usual makeup, but took extra time with her hair, coiling it high on her head and securing it with rhinestone pins. Tonight, was important for the Belliveaus'. Sliding into a pair of matching, lilac-coloured, strappy sandals, she bent to pull the backs over her heels and straightened with a sigh of satisfaction. She pushed open her same bedroom door from her first visit and descended the staircase.

There wasn't the usual chatter from the dining room and Angelina glanced at her watch, wondering if she was too early. She adjusted her course to wait on the terrace. The sliding French doors were open, and she glided through, then halted in her tracks.

A small, round table was set for two by the pool. A white cloth covering gleamed under a full moon and the crystal glasses and silverware sparkled beside tall flickering candles.

Julien moved toward her from the shadows carrying a white trumpet-like flower by a long stem.

"A moon flower," Angelina breathed. As he approached, she looked into his dark eyes and felt her heart surge with love for this man.

"*Oui, mademoiselle.*" His voice was husky. He stopped before her, his spicy cologne playing havoc with her mind. Reaching out, he gently pulled the two pins from her hair and caught the silky curls as they cascaded around her shoulders.

"*Désolé*," he said, his eyes smoldering like coals. "Your hairstyle was beautiful. Perfect for an evening out on the town, but I love it to be loose and caressing your shoulders when you are alone with me." He tucked the moon flower behind her ear and his fingertips brushed her neck as they traced a path across her skin to cup her chin and lift her face to his. His lips followed, claiming hers in a kiss that left her weak.

"The flower is lovely," he continued. "But you, my dearest Angelina, are gorgeous. I love you more with each day that passes."

"You do?" Angelina whispered.

He smiled. "I do. And, although I planned to wait until after our dessert, I find that I cannot." His hands fell away as he reached into a pocket of the dark suit he wore; his eyes never leaving hers.

The terrace was only dimly lit, aided in part by a chandelier inside the chateau. Yet Angelina could see that his face was flushed and hopeful when he snapped open a small, red-velvet box on the palm of his hand.

Inside, diamonds glittered. Angelina flung a hand to her mouth to stifle a gasp. She looked at Julien, comprehension dawning on her face like silvery tendrils of the moon rising from the clouds.

"Will you marry me, Angelina?" he asked, saying her name in the French accent she loved so well. "Will you share your life with me in France and set your roots into the soil of Provence?"

"Yes."

It was only one, tiny, three-letter word. But it was packed with a lifetime of love and commitment as she leaned forward to kiss his lips lingeringly.

He eased the ring from its box and took Angelina's hand. Sliding it onto her finger they admired it for a moment before Julien circled her waist with his arm and, unheeded, the box dropped to the flagstones beneath their feet.

Emotions threatened to overwhelm Angelina. She had found the love of her life in a land that she adored. Who could have ever guessed?

She moved into the circle of his loving embrace as the scented night air swirled about them, sanctifying their love.

Angelina had found everything in Provence she didn't know she'd been looking for. It had truly become one golden summer.

If you enjoyed this book, it would mean so very much to me if you would leave a review. Thank you!

Ready for more romance? Get **Moonlight Over the Cinque Terre**.

JOIN MY MONTHLY NEWSLETTER FOR ALL THE LATEST news.

JOIN MY NEWSLETTER

Interested in hearing more about my books and upcoming releases? Be sure to sign up for my newsletter at **https://helentoews.com/newsletter** *so you don't miss a beat.*

ABOUT THE AUTHOR

Helen Row Toews is an author and humourist, works as EA and school bus driver, and carries a license to drive anything on wheels. She grew up and still resides on the family farm near Marshall, Saskatchewan, where Charolais cattle and gophers flourish (the latter being purely coincidental and highly unappreciated). She's been blessed with four grown children and two grandchildren that bring her endless joy.

Helen loves the prairies and its people. She feels privileged to take her readers on exciting adventures in the Runestaff Chronicles series and to bring her readers a smile with her columns and books entitled Prairie Wool.

Printed in Great Britain
by Amazon